# TIDES OF WAR

DROWNED EARTH

# DROWNED EARTH

**Eight novellas.**
**Eight Australian authors.**
**One watery apocalypse.**

Scientists said that it would take 5000 years for Earth's
oceans to rise.

They were wrong.

After an asteroid collides with Antarctica, a tsunami
devastates the world's coastal cities and escalates the melting
of the ice caps.

These eight novellas set in various locations around Australia
explore the potential consequences of such a catastrophe.
They can be read in any order.

Prequel short story: Shards of Silver by Alanah Andrews
The Rise by Sue-Ellen Pashley
Fire Over Troubled Water by Nick Marone
Submerged City by Austin P. Sheehan
Tides of War by Marcus Turner
The Jindabyne Secret by Jo Hart
River of Diamonds by S. M. Isaac
Salvaged by C.A. Clark
Emoto's Promise by Shel Calopa

# TIDES OF WAR

## MARCUS TURNER

DROWNED EARTH

First published by Deadset Press in 2019

www.aussiespeculativefiction.com

ISBN: 978-0-6484211-7-7

Cover design Copyright © Alanah Andrews

Edited by Alanah Andrews & Austin P. Sheehan

www.aussiespeculativefiction.com

# DEDICATION

*For Tita:*

*For all your loving support, and your mad courage in marrying a writer.*

# CHAPTER ONE

The broken and rusting towers rose on the horizon like a bony hand, the skeletal claw of civilisation reaching up out of the waters. The sea gleamed like an obsidian mirror, and the remaining panes of glass in the towers intensified the morning glare, burning Maria's retinas even through her tinted goggles.

Maria hated coming to the Reef. She kept arguing with Vishal that it was pointless combing over the ruins—they'd already been looted bare—plus it was becoming too dangerous. Just last week, Callaghan's boat hit a submerged tram with its back end rearing up. Salvagers found the wreck, but not the bodies of Callaghan's crew. Powerful eddying currents, contaminated water, too many places for pirates and raiders to hide for ambush. The fisherfolk had stopped coming, and yet the scavengers ploughed on.

But desperate times called for desperate measures. She knew the dangerous journey was necessary. Her home, Endurance Point, was slowly starving. The past year's crops had failed—Jeff reckoned the soil had finally become too salty to yield crops—forcing them to dig into their stored reserves. The fishers were under immense pressure to deliver *the miracle* catch, but it never seemed to come. Vishal insisted it would, if they kept trying—but what would he know? He never went out on the water, didn't know the conditions—too busy handing out the marching orders. Meanwhile, Maria and the other scavs were sent out to pick over bare bones, these tetanus-riddled hellholes.

She gazed about the exposed towers as she slid past the ruins of Aurora Tower. Violent storms and tsunamis had made broken teeth of the skyscrapers and apartment buildings jutting out of the sea, but some of the damage was new. Plate glass windows glared back as shattered black eyes where harsh white sun-fire had flared only days earlier. *Looters.* Other survivors were getting desperate, too.

She rowed past the empty spot where the Rialto Towers once stood, past the tips of rusting icebergs jutting from the water—the soaring, scarred frame of Eureka Tower soon looming above her. Beyond the Reef, to the south, lay the glimmering black plain of Hidden Bay.

A sunken city below her feet. A modern-day Atlantis, taken back by the ocean.

If only memories, and pain, drowned as easily as cities.

Normally, the Bay teemed with fisherfolk from settlements all along the Southern Seaboard, arriving well before dawn. Yet today the Bay was empty, the fisherfolk still in their beds or fishing elsewhere. Perhaps it had provided its last healthy morsel, the contamination finally spread to all living creatures—or, more likely, pirates prowled the waters.

Maria surveyed the horizon. With the Mornington and Bellarine Peninsulas both underwater, a vast, borderless gulf stretched in either direction for hundreds of kilometres. Except for a few rusting tankers drifting like luxury liners for the dead, there was nowhere for pirates to hide, except in the maze of the Reef.

After a few moments, she let out a relieved breath, then began to gather her equipment—her backpack, her grappling hook and rope, and her pistol holstered beneath her seat. One could never be too careful.

Maria tested an exposed bit of metal protruding from a mangled window frame just above the water line; satisfied it wouldn't snap off, she moored her dinghy to it, then threw her hook up to the sagging edge of the floor above. To her relief, it didn't give when she put her weight on it.

Her limbs burned as she shimmied up the rope. It was a long way to the top, and a lot of floors to cover before dusk.

\*\*\*

Maria arrived back at camp an hour after sunset, gliding the boat towards the small jetty. She did not get out straight away—the gentle rocking of the tide was almost like a lullaby. She could have easily laid down and let herself fall asleep, but it wasn't the exhaustion alone—it was also the sight at the bottom of her boat, the near empty backpack by her feet, that caused her to procrastinate. Vishal wasn't going to be happy.

She knew the others in the camp would try to be sympathetic, understanding the reality, but she could already hear the whispers in their private thoughts. *Maria Beaumont, the lazy, inept scav.*

She moored the dinghy and stepped onto the jetty. The walk was long, normally well-lit by flaming torches, except a few had already guttered out. The fences, rising nearly twenty feet high, doubled the gloom, blocking the glow of the bonfire behind them. *They've really got to stop this*, she thought miserably. It wouldn't be long before firewood became another item added to the ever-increasing list of dangerously low supplies. They'd cut down most of the large trees in the surrounding area just to make the fences. Endurance Point only occupied about a one-kilometre square space, the largest island at the centre of a wide delta that had formed along the northernmost part of the old Craigieburn suburbs. A short ford stood at the settlement's northern border, a shallow crossing to the mainland.

Before the Rise, the area had been undeveloped. Now, the surrounding land for kilometres in either direction was almost entirely bare, cleared of trees except for small, stunted saplings and squat, hardy bush.

Considering the dire priority of growing or obtaining food, having to gather firewood for a bonfire that nobody really needed seemed an unnecessary waste of resources. Of course, maybe necessity wasn't the point—the bonfire was a beacon of hope, a symbol of camp morale.

*Fucking Jagannatha.* The damned asteroid had brought about a second flood worthy of the Bible, but unlike Noah's, there was little hope of a dove coming back with the promise of plenty. Jagannatha had made certain that inland Australia would become nothing less than Hell on earth, salted ground girt by capricious seas. The spitefully named "Lord of the Universe" had taken everything, bit by bit.

*No. Can't blame everything on Jagannatha. This is people's fault. Our fault.*

Maria nodded at Darryl, the guard on duty, then headed through the gates. The heat from the bonfire enveloped her like an ethereal hug, driving the chill from her bones. Maybe the fire wasn't a necessity, but it certainly was welcome. She crossed the courtyard, darting out of the way as a group of young children raced around the fire laughing, then headed towards the kitchen—a small, open-air kiosk with a rough-hewn bench and a corrugated steel roof. A massive copper kettle hung over a small rock fireplace on the ground, glowing dimly.

Jeff, the cook and *de facto* quartermaster, was hunkered down beside the kettle, cursing to himself and trying to get the fire to liven up. Maria smirked. Jeff was a hell of a cook, but he was a shitty outdoorsman.

"Hey, Jeff."

"Hi, Maria," Jeff replied without looking up. "Let me guess—came up empty."

"Better than expected."

"Which, I'm guessing, still means *shit*."

Maria sighed. "Yep."

Jeff looked up at her, frowning. "Shit."

"I keep telling Vishal we need to explore elsewhere. He won't listen."

"Yeah, well, you know politicians." Jeff turned back to the kindling and blew on it a few times, the embers flaring brighter. "Apparently the new wave hasn't learned anything from the old. Then again, how could they, with them all at the bottom of the sea?"

"Wish he'd take a jump and join 'em."

"He's alright. He's doing his best, just like you." The cooking fire was finally starting to catch. Jeff pulled his face away from the curling flames and stopped blowing. "So, what'd you find today?"

Maria dumped the contents of her backpack on the counter. A small bag of basmati rice she'd found underneath one of the market shelves; three toilet paper rolls that looked like they'd been gnawed on by a rat; three small spice shakers containing paprika, rosemary and taco seasoning.

Jeff looked as if he'd been slapped. "You're kidding."

"Afraid not."

"Jesus Christ, Maria."

"It's not *my* bloody fault—" she hissed.

"I know, but Christ . . ." Jeff shook his head, then

picked up the paprika. "Well, at least now maybe I can add some flavour to the crap I cook."

Maria grinned. "Got any smoke?"

"*Shhh!*" Jeff raised a finger to his lips. "I don't want anyone knowing I've been sneaking it. Christ. The one thing we've got that'll keep for trade. If Vishal finds out I've been flogging it, that *we've* been smoking it—"

"Will you relax?" Maria smiled. "He's not going to miss a few buds."

"He will since we can't grow any more and all we've got is what's dried up in storage."

"Well? Do you have any or don't you?" she demanded impatiently.

Jeff rolled his eyes and turned away. "Yes, I've got smoke. Is that the only reason you love me?"

"No, not the only reason."

Jeff scoffed. "For a mature quail, you're pretty savage, you know that?"

"Why do you think I like the smoke?" She laughed, tipping him a wink. "Dulls my edges a bit."

"Maybe we can push the twin beds together tonight?"

"Hey"—Maria jabbed a finger at him, suppressing a smile—"don't you get fresh with me, smart guy."

She turned and left Jeff, grinning, to finish

cooking the evening meal, and headed to sit by the bonfire. Then someone called out, "*Maria!*"

She groaned and turned around to see Vishal walking over, hands already placed on his hips.

"Yes, Vishal?"

"Guessing the pickings weren't great today?" he said, narrowing his eyes, as if he wanted to say something else, something insulting.

"You'd be right, of course," she said, gesturing towards Jeff's bench where the items still stood. "But then I've been telling you that for weeks. *Months.* The Reef's picked clean."

"I don't think so," he replied curtly.

"That's because you've never been."

"I'm reassigning you," Vishal said abruptly, pursing his lips.

"What?"

"You're not producing results. I think there might be others better equipped to go on scav missions."

"Vishal," Maria said quietly through her teeth, "if you just listened to me and sent our teams to explore new ground, we might actually find something."

"Wake up, Maria. Don't blame the other teams, or the Reef. We both know why you don't produce the goods. We know what happened there, to Luke—"

*"Don't you dare mention his name!"* Maria growled,

her raised voice drawing the attention of people nearby.

"Point is, there's a conflict of interest here, and I think it would be best if someone else took over your scav position. All right?"

Maria exhaled loudly, nostrils flaring. "So, what are you reassigning me to?"

"For the moment, fishing. Ramirez and Amirah are both sick, so we need a couple of extras out in the blue. I know you're good out on the water, know how to handle a boat, how to fish."

Maria made an annoyed sound. "This is bullshit, Vishal. This has nothing to do with Luke and you know it—"

"It's my decision. Either do it, or you can fuck off and live somewhere else. Oh, and by the way"—he leaned in close, their faces inches apart—"if you ever go off at me in front of the others again, I'll have you thrown out so fast your neck will break from the spin. Understand?"

"Yeah, I get the picture," Maria growled, but Vishal had already stormed off towards his cabin.

# CHAPTER TWO

The dark water glimmered beneath the hot sun, diamonds sparkling along its surface. The boat rocked gently in the calm water, but Maria felt ill at ease being so far out. She'd seen first-hand how quickly things could change; how benign white clouds and blue skies could give way to sudden, vicious squalls and monstrous thunderheads as black as coal.

But she enjoyed the quiet, the isolation. She could be less guarded here, both physically and mentally. The Reef stirred up too many bad memories. She hadn't been out there when the tsunami hit—but she could imagine what it had been like. Luke had been working in the city that day when Jagannatha arrived, working maintenance on the NBN lines beneath the ground. He never came home. He never got the warning.

Maria pushed the invading thoughts from her mind and closed her eyes, focusing on the squawk of the gulls, the water sloshing against the sides of the boat. *Be present. Breathe. Hold. Release. Be present.*

A strong tug beneath the water bent the big rod like a bowstring. Maria jerked the rod upwards and spun the reel with practised dexterity. After a brief struggle, she pulled the line clear of the water. A long silvery fish thrashed about on the hook. A King George whiting— not bad. Decent size, though they didn't taste the best. They had a slightly unpleasant metallic taste—but at least it'd be safe to eat, free of contamination this far out beyond the Bay.

She unhooked the fish and then stuffed it into the net with the others. Today had been a decent catch— nine fish so far. Maybe Vishal was right about her being in the wrong niche—just not the *why* of it. Sonofabitch. That was a low blow, bringing Luke up. If he'd said a word about Abby or Deon, she'd have socked him right in—

A dark smudge bobbing on the ocean's surface caught her eye. She squinted, trying to make it out, then reached for her binoculars.

A boat, black with red striped panelling, floating

to the south.

Maria grabbed the revolver beneath her seat. The boat was moving slowly—it didn't seem to have its motor running and it was just bobbing along with the swell. She couldn't see anyone inside.

*An ambush,* she thought . . . But there were no other boats out on the water, not that she could see. There was nowhere to hide out here; even if it were an ambush, she'd see them coming from ages away.

She watched the boat for several minutes, her limbs taut, her senses keen as a butcher's blade. The boat did not move any faster and nobody appeared. A lone curious seagull landed upon the black boat's prow, peering inside. Maria finally slid the revolver back in its holster, put the binoculars down and fired up the motor.

The seagull took flight as she trundled closer. It was not some old, dented dinghy. It was brand new, top of the line. There was no manufacturer's mark, no company logo; it had no scratches or any discernible identification on its plain black surfaces. An odd sort of shape—a pentagonal prow, a long, tapered hull, a trapezoidal stern. Carbon fibre—must have been worth a fortune. An expensive thing to lose out at sea. Maybe Maria could finally get an upgrade, if there was still fuel in the tank and functioning equipment . . .

But as she stood up, ready to make the short leap

13

across, she realised the boat was not as unoccupied as it seemed.

Lying on the deck, obscured by the low gunwales, was a hideously sunburnt, bruised man, naked except for a pair of urine-stained underwear.

Maria watched him for a long moment, prepared to flee at full throttle if he suddenly shot up to attack.

He didn't move.

Realising he was unconscious, his breathing shallow, Maria grabbed the coil of blue rope from the footwell and tied one end to the U-bolt in her bow, before leaping into the other vessel, landing a few feet from the man's body. She scrutinised him warily, gun drawn, as she secured the other end of the rope to the black boat's bow.

Then she approached the man slowly, kneeling and laying two fingers on the side of his neck. His pulse was as faint as butterfly wings. His skin was lobster red and peeling; his lips shrivelled and cracked like broken clay. Hard to say how long he'd been out here, or what he'd been doing—there were no nets, no fishing rods, no personal artefacts, no sign even of his clothes.

Maria got up to check the fuel gauge. The needle sat on empty. So he'd run out of fuel. How long ago? It still didn't answer what he'd been doing out here. It was possible he'd run afoul of pirates, been beaten and

14

robbed of everything except for his undies, and left to die out under the unforgiving sun. That's exactly the sort of thing the raiders liked to do; a bit of a game for them. But something about that didn't sit right. *If it'd been pirates, surely they would have taken the boat.*

"Hey!" Maria shouted, shaking the man by the shoulder. He let out a long, delirious moan, shifting his head drunkenly. His eyeballs fluttered beneath red-purple lids. "*Hey*! Can you hear me?" She shook harder, which drew a louder, pained groan. She glanced at her hand pressing down on his beetroot shoulder and pulled it away.

"Hang on, I'm gonna get you out of here." She unbuttoned her shirt, leaving herself dressed in only a grubby white singlet, and covered him as best she could from the sun's rays. Even the light cotton material against his skin seemed to cause pain, as he writhed on the floor of his boat. Still, she hoped it would give him some relief.

She wanted to move the man into her own ship, but was afraid to try to shift him.

"Hang on, mate, I'm going to get you help. Take you some place safe."

Maria jumped back into her boat, started the motor, and turned it back towards the Bay, the black boat and its dying passenger following in her wake.

.

# CHAPTER THREE

"What the hell did you think you were doing?"

Maria turned from the sleeping stranger and fixed her gaze on Vishal. "The right thing."

"You don't even know who he is!" Vishal snarled. "He could be bloody anybody!"

"He looks like a victim to me. I decided to help him."

"At what cost to the community?"

"Oh, get stuffed," Maria snapped, shaking her head. "A bit of food and medicine is a small price to pay for human decency—"

"You're out of line. We're digging into our reserves at it is. What we can afford to give isn't a call you get to make." Vishal jabbed a finger at his own chest. "I call the shots around here, not you."

Maria sneered. "Nonetheless. My conscious is clear. Is yours?"

"This isn't over." The look of pure loathing he gave her before stalking out of the dark infirmary was prophetic: he was going to exile her. *Or at least try to.*

"How's he doing, Nat?" Maria asked, pushing the thought away.

Natalia, the young Pole playing camp nurse, wore a worried expression. "I'm doing the best I can. I've given him Panadol to try to bring his fever down—but so far it isn't working, and I don't have a lot left. I'm giving him sips of water, but what we really need are electrolyte drinks—Gastrolyte, Gatorade—which we don't have."

"We could—"

"Don't even say scavenging mission," Natalia told her sternly. "You're in enough trouble already— plus, you've been kicked off the scav team. Vishal will never go for it. Not for an outsider." She held her fingers over the stranger's left wrist and frowned. "His heartbeat is still very weak."

"Has he regained consciousness at all?" Maria asked.

Natalia shook her head. "Just enough to take water and meds. Occasionally he'll mumble stuff, but it's gibberish. He's delirious."

"What do you think his chances are?"

Natalia's gaze was direct, solemn. "I don't even want to say."

For the next three days, Maria departed before the sun rose, crossed the Reef and Hidden Bay and headed out into the big blue. After each fishing day, she returned to the infirmary to check in on the sun-ravaged stranger. His condition seemed to change very little, but Natalia assured her he was slowly improving.

"He's taking more fluid and keeping it down," Natalia said. "First few days he was throwing up as much as he took down. He's also staying awake for longer and his heartbeat has stabilised, nice and strong." She smiled. "He'll make it."

On the fourth night, following a relatively lacklustre day of fishing, Maria walked into the infirmary to find the stranger awake, sitting upright in bed.

"Oh," she said, taken aback. "Hi."

His lucid eyes regarded her coolly; the scalded-red colour of his skin had finally started to subside, the damaged skin beginning to peel. Natalia was nowhere in sight. Darryl was sitting in the chair in the corner, his gun resting in his lap.

Maria nodded when their eyes met. "Where's Nat?"

"Gone out for some food," Darryl replied.

"What are you doing here?"

"Gotta watch the newcomer. Vishal's orders."

"I hardly think you need to worry—"

"I'm flattered," a male voice interjected, gravelly from disuse, "that you feel my presence requires a personal security detail."

Maria and Darryl glanced at the stranger and then back at each other.

"I hear I have you to thank for saving my life," he said, addressing Maria.

"I was one who found you. But Natalia has done all the heavy lifting since."

"Still . . . Thanks."

Maria tilted her head graciously, smiling. "I'm Maria."

"Richard Campbell."

"Richard, what were you doing out there?"

There was a long pause. He bit his lip and shifted uncomfortably.

"Were you attacked? Was it pirates?"

Richard took a deep breath. "I was left out there to die."

"By whom?"

Richard met Maria's gaze with apprehensive eyes. "You wouldn't believe me if I told you."

"Try me."

"Can I—Can I speak to you, privately?" Richard was looking at Darryl's gun nervously.

"Darryl, could you give us a few minutes?"

"I'm under strict—" Darryl started.

"I won't tell if you won't tell." Her voice softened, placating. "Please. I'll be fine, I promise."

Darryl grimaced, but then he reluctantly nodded, rose and went towards the tent flaps. "Five minutes. I'll be outside the door."

"Thanks, Darryl."

Maria turned back to Richard. "What is it?"

"Someone did try to kill me," Richard said quietly, looking at his feet.

"I already gathered that. Who? Why?"

Richard hesitated. "I was exiled."

"Why?"

"A coup. I led a coup against the leadership, and we were routed. The other insurgents were all executed; the leaders took away my clothes and put me out to sea with minimal fuel, no food or water. It was still a death sentence. They wanted to make an example out of me."

Maria frowned. That didn't sound like a sentence any of the Bay communities would mete out—not even East Prom. Nor had she heard of any coups on the grapevine. "Which settlement were you exiled from, exactly? The Marsh? Kurunjang Port? East Prom?"

Richard averted his gaze. "None of those."

"Where, then?"

"Nowhere on the land," he answered, looking at her earnestly.

An antarctic chill crept through Maria's skin. "Nowhere on land? I don't understand. What are you trying to tell me?"

Richard took a deep breath. "I come from a city, but not on land. A secret city hidden out at sea."

# CHAPTER FOUR

"Come again?"

Richard sighed. "You don't believe me."

"No, I don't believe you," Maria said, arms folding across her chest. "It's just not possible."

"Why's it not possible?"

"Oh, come on! A city out at sea? You're telling me there's a secret city nobody knows about, except you, somewhere out in the blue?"

"I'm telling the truth."

"We have fishers going out into the blue every day, from every community. If there was a city out at sea, someone would have seen and reported them."

Richard shook his head. "They're nowhere near

the land, and they're way outside even the furthest ranges your fisherfolk go."

"*They?* You're saying there's more than one?"

"Plenty more, all around Australia—all around the world."

Maria violently shook her head, seething. "So you're saying people built these cities after Jagannatha, after the Rise? I don't even know where to start pointing out the flaws with that."

"I didn't say that. They weren't built after the Rise. They were built *before*, as a contingency: a secret government project between friendly nations, designed and built for a cataclysm such as this—"

"You sound like a tinfoil-wearing conspiracy nut, you know that?"

Richard smiled. "And you lack imagination."

Maria scoffed. "A secret government project, huh? Okay, I'll bite. Tell me."

"The lotus cities—that's what they call them— were specially designed to withstand an ecological apocalypse. They're tsunami- and hurricane-resistant, able to cope with hammerings that a fixed city could not. They are mobile. They run on solar and hydroelectric power, pumping water up through an underwater root system to spin the turbines. Desalination plants for near unlimited clean water. Food stores that could sustain the entire populace on-board for between fifty to a hundred years; drag-nets for fresh seafood every day. Advanced weapon systems and defensive capabilities, long-range radar. You have to understand, these things are built to sustain the populace under *any* circumstance. They're arks, in a sense—ensuring the preservation of the human race."

"Where are they located?"

Richard shrugged. "Hard to say. They could be anywhere now. Before Jagannatha, they were way out in the Tasman, the Bight, the Pacific, far from islands and the coast. The one I come from is called Atlas-3, and it's the closest to the mainland, located in the middle of Bass Strait. Though it could have migrated elsewhere by now."

Maria scrunched her face sceptically. "So you're saying the government secretly built these lotus cities, without anybody knowing, put them out to sea—"

"No, they built them out at sea, far from prying eyes."

"Right. And then they relocated to these cities just in time for the tsunamis?"

"No," Richard said. "They were already aboard the cities long before Jagannatha arrived."

"*What?*" Maria said incredulously. "But—But that would mean . . ."

"The government knew in advance that

Jagannatha was coming and was going to hit Antarctica. And they didn't say anything."

Maria stared at him for a long time, unable to speak. Then she let out a short laugh. "There's a fatal flaw with your story: the government was wiped out. Everybody knows that. Nobody's heard from them since the tsunamis stopped. They're either disbanded or dead. They're *gone*."

"Is that what you think?" Richard raised an eyebrow, wearing a ghost of a smile. "You dare only imagine a government that looks out for its people, its country—but deep down, surely you must know the truth."

"What truth might that be?"

Richard leaned forward. "That the government, the wealthy and powerful don't give a shit about you, or anybody else. That's what the lotus city contingency was all about: protecting their own asses, while everybody else died, or was left to die slowly."

"No," Maria said, shaking her head, "that's just not possible."

"*How* is it not possible?"

"It just isn't!" Maria shouted. "How could a government just uproot and flee without anybody knowing?"

"The country was in disarray after the asteroid

hit. The entire world was, but we copped it worst of all. NASA and the other space agencies had been keeping a close eye on the meteor shower—they even told the public about it. What they didn't say—what they all agreed not to say—was that Jagannatha, the *Lord of the Universe*, was going to strike Antarctica."

"Why wouldn't they say anything?" Maria's voice was barely a whisper.

"They knew the situation was untenable. They couldn't save everybody. They didn't want to risk a panic."

"Why didn't the other nations help us?"

"The information was deemed classified. To admit they all knew and allowed a key world nation to collapse would be to accept culpability for everything else that would follow in their own countries—to invite the wrath of the people. It was easier for the government to play dead and disband, and the international community to turn a blind eye.

"NASA and their international colleagues projected the fallout of Jagannatha's impact and the accelerated melt, and the ripple effect it would have around the world. They, much later than us, began to create lotus cities of their own, for when the full force of the Rise made a ruin of their own homelands. I don't think even in their projections they understood how rapidly everything would unravel."

Maria's head felt like it was going to explode into bloody confetti. All this new knowledge—it was too much. It was only the sober sincerity in Richard's voice that kept her will to deny his story as an elaborate lie at bay.

"The government fled, and left everybody else behind," she said flatly, her voice frosty.

"And not just the government," Richard said, "but all their rich, powerful friends. They warned them in advance. Days prior to the impact, members of the federal government—and select state allies—and their rich pals boarded ships bound for lotus cities around the country. When Jagannatha hit and the tsunamis began streaking up from the Antarctic, they were already safely aboard."

Maria looked down at her hands, which were trembling. Luke, and so many other unsuspecting people that day—sentenced to death without a thought. Numbness prickled across her body—she felt disjointed, outside herself.

And everything that followed—Abby, Deon; her parents, her friends, all succumbed to Jagannatha and the Rise by degrees . . .

"They didn't care," Maria said.

"No. Or maybe they did care, but they just cared

more about themselves. A city of privilege, wanting for nothing, hoarding technology and the means to save thousands, millions of lives—reserved entirely for the wealthy, the politically powerful, while the rest of you fight over the scraps of a ruined world, to starve, thirst and kill each other." Richard held her gaze with dark, hypnotising eyes. "Business as usual, even while the world ends."

Maria was silent for several moments. "Why were you aboard?"

Richard sighed. "At the time of the Rise I was a secretary for the Minister of Defence," he said. "Until that position, along with the former positions of government, were dissolved. But I was fortunate enough to be among a select few government employees to be given a golden ticket during the exodus."

All at once, the enormity of the revelations—the great weight of truth crushing the small pockets of resistance and denial within her—came rushing in with the force of that first tsunami. Her husband, Luke, working in some closet-sized hole underground, tinkering with wires, swallowed by the surging seas. Did he even know what was happening? Her children, herself, all slowly starving, before she ever found Endurance Point. Deon, passing in his sleep, complications of pneumonia, for which they couldn't find any medicine to treat. Abby, dying in whimpering agony from dysentery. So much regret, so much *failure*. How they had suffered, how she had suffered, before she found Endurance Point. *Too late by then,* she thought bitterly. But the lotus cities—they could have saved them, saved everybody . . .

All this heartache, all this loss—because of *them*, those smug, rich bastards who thought the unwashed masses were unworthy of the gift of life.

"You're one of them," Maria said accusingly.

"I was never one of them," Richard retorted, eyes narrowed. "I fought against them, after a while. I was *exiled* for it, remember?"

"No, you're one of them." Maria shook her head, her face hardening as tears welled in her eyes. "I should have left you to rot out in the blue."

"Maria—" he called after her, but she was already out the door before he had even finished uttering her name.

\*\*\*

She surged through the darkness, wiping her eyes with the back of her hand as she beelined towards Vishal's hut. She had to tell him. She wasn't about to protect someone complicit in the hardship of thousands, perhaps millions of survivors across the continent, left to fend for themselves while the cowardly oligarchs fled instead of picking up the pieces.

No wonder no help had ever come. Once the Rise had claimed the old coast and the new inland sea had come rushing in, they must have realised it was too expensive, too immense an undertaking to rebuild the nation's infrastructure. Melbourne, Sydney, Brisbane, Adelaide, Perth, all underwater—probably figured there was no point. *Untenable*—that's the word Richard used.

*They knew . . . they fucking knew . . .* Maria couldn't believe the arrogance of it, *the judgement* the few had swung like an executioner's axe. That Australians had come up with the model for protecting the oligarchs, the corporate powerhouses—that they knew how the loss of Antarctica would destabilise the global climate and expedite the global ice melt.

Now Antarctica, the Arctic, Greenland, Siberia, all the glaciers were gone. Nothing would have stopped Jagannatha, nor the global melt—but they could have still *warned* people; helped people onto those lotus cities. Instead they left them all behind, gods among mere men, leaving the unworthy to drown in the next Great Flood.

She felt something dark swell within her, a switch that killed the light, the potential and memory of joy . . . A black rage that threatened to eclipse their faces in hellish shadow forever.

*Vishal,* she thought. *For all our differences, you will want to know about this. You will be angry, and together we will act. You have to.*

Maria reached his wooden hut and threw the door open. Vishal, sitting with his feet up on his weather-beaten desk, only looked mildly surprised at her sweaty, flustered entrance. "Maria," he said sardonically. "What a pleasant surprise."

"Spare me the affectations, Vishal," she said. "I need you to set aside your dislike for me for a moment and listen."

Vishal flashed her a thin, unpleasant smile. "I don't dislike you, Maria—"

"Cut the crap. I need to tell you something. Something big and . . . frankly, unbelievable. I hardly believe it myself."

Vishal took his legs off the desk and leaned forward on his elbows. "Sounds serious."

"It is," she said, ignoring his sarcasm. "It's about the new guy."

Vishal's eyebrows rose and he leant back in his chair, scowling. "Ah. Him."

"He told me a story you wouldn't believe, about where he came from, about . . . About a bunch of secret oceanic cities harbouring the government and the wealthy."

Vishal gazed at her for a moment before a grin broke on his face. "You're pulling my leg, aren't you?"

"I know what it sounds like," she replied peevishly. "I didn't believe it myself at first. I'm still not entirely sure I do. But a lot of what he says . . . The pieces all fit, Vishal. Why the government didn't sweep in to help, clean-up or rebuild after the disaster; why they just dropped"—her hands made a loud *crack* as she clapped them together—"off the radar. We thought they all died. That was the rumour going around between the communities anyway. Except then I remembered: I went to Canberra once, a long time ago—and there's no way it got flooded. It never occurred to me until I heard Richard's story. Canberra is way above current sea level, and there's no way even the massive wave straight after Jagannatha would have gone that far inland."

"Oceanic cities, you say? Reserved for government? Am I hearing you right so far?"

Maria nodded. "And their rich friends. Richard claims he was a secretary for the Minister of Defence. Said the government and their buddies knew about the meteor well in advance and didn't tell the public to avoid a panic. That's why they had the meteor alert downgraded. You remember?"

Vishal nodded. "I remember."

"So before Jagannatha had even struck

Antarctica, they had already boarded the lotus cities, safe and sound."

Vishal mulled over Maria's recount for a while, nodding thoughtfully. "That's quite a tale," he said. "Quite fanciful and complex for a man not long coming out of delirium."

Maria sighed. "Vishal, I think you need to take this seriously."

"Oh, I am," he snapped. "I am. You don't perform, you don't contribute the same as the others—"

"That is *bullshit*—"

"—you undermine me in front of the other campers, making it open season on the leadership—then you bring a goddamned *lunatic* into our midst—"

"Vishal, he says he was exiled from this place, one of the cities out there in Bass Strait."

"Exiled?" Vishal gave a curt laugh. "Even better? Another low-life among us."

"Get stuffed," Maria growled, turning away.

"Let's suppose his story is true for a second," Vishal called after her, and she stopped. "At what fucking point did you think harbouring an exile was a smart move? Huh? You don't even know who he is, except what he tells you!"

"Vishal, I don't think—"

"No, you don't. You rarely do?" His mouth was

a hard slash, smoothing his face into a stone death-mask. "We take care of our own at Endurance Point, our own above all others. But you forget that. You live in your own quagmire of bitterness and self-loathing and meanwhile, the people around you suffer." Vishal threw up his hands. "What were you expecting when you decided to come tell me this story? I've gotta know."

"I thought maybe you'd get angry. I thought you might think of all the people lost, all the people *we've* lost, all because rich assholes thought themselves more deserving than the rest of us. And then maybe, just maybe, you'd *do something about it.*"

"You're damned right I'm angry," Vishal replied. "And I am doing something."

Maria regarded him with a puzzled expression.

"Enjoy your last night at Endurance Point, because at sunrise tomorrow, you *and* him are *both* exiled from this camp."

# CHAPTER FIVE

"Jesus Christ," Jeff said, shaking his head.

Maria took a long drag of the joint, coughed and screwed up her face, before passing it back. "Tell me about it."

"Do you believe him?"

"I don't know." Maria was nestled high above the camp in an unmanned watch tower, staring at the horizon, watching the black slowly ebb to Prussian blue. "It's pretty hard to, but then, it's hard not to. He truly believed what he said, I could see that."

"Maybe he's nuts. Delirious."

"Maybe."

"Was it worth getting exiled over?" Jeff asked,

deadpan.

"No idea. Won't know until I have proof."

"Proof?"

Maria took another drag, exhaled, then screwed up her face again and stuck out her tongue. "Ugh. I don't want any more of that."

Jeff shrugged again. "More for me."

"I don't know," Maria said, sighing. "See with my own eyes, I guess. Break a piece off. Who knows? Maybe it was pointless. This whole thing has just shredded my brain."

"The weed's probably not helping."

"No . . . It is. Believe that."

"Maybe you need some sleep, old girl. I definitely do."

Maria sighed, stretching her arms and torso. Then she scowled. "Who are you calling *old girl*, shit-stain?" She laughed at Jeff's expression of shock.

"Maria, you don't swear!"

"Well, then, don't call me old girl. I can still knock the cheek out of you."

"I'd rather a trip around the world, if you take my meaning," Jeff said with a sly wink.

Maria watched a furtive little smile break upon his face, an inciting gleam in his periwinkle eyes. She shot to her feet, a little too fast; she had to steady herself as the blood rushed to her head. The marijuana haze cleared after a moment.

"Mind out of the gutter, Jeff. I'm married."

"Well, not really—"

"I know what you're going to say, Jeff," she said, waving her wedding ring in front of her face, before she clambered down the ladder. "Still married."

"I'm sure Luke wouldn't mind," she heard Jeff grumble.

***

Maria sat on the bed, weariness stealing over her body and mind. The weed was working its magic, pulling her inexorably towards a dreamless slumber. The nights she hung out with Jeff and shared a scoob had become more regular in the past year.

The old her would have despised the new for smoking, let alone smoking green—but then the old her never had to cope with recurring nightmares of her dead children and husband.

She reached down under the bed and retrieved the battered shoebox containing her few precious possessions. A set of now useless keys to the Astra convertible Luke had bought as a gift for her 40th birthday. A Zippo lighter Jeff had given her about a year ago, stamped with a flaming horned skull on the side—a memento from the days before.

And her battered purse, filled with useless plastic cards, and a clear plastic window with a photo: the last Christmas before Jagannatha—Abigail and Deon, beaming down the lens, Deon flashing his newly unwrapped Beyblade, while Luke grinned over Deon's shoulder.

She zipped the purse back up, tossed it into the box and slid it back under her bed. Why did she do this to herself, every night?

*Because I'm forgetting their faces,* she thought, blinking away a tear. *I can't remember what they look like without it. Time is bleaching their pictures.*

She sat for a moment longer, trying to exhale the pain before she laid down to sleep. But it refused to yield. The pain turned inside her belly, disquieted, sadness and loss becoming a dance of knives, hot and sharp, scaling the length of her insides.

Her scalp prickled with rage, and her knuckles turned white as they tightened around the wooden bedframe.

\*\*\*

"Richard, wake up."

Richard stirred, half-turned. Maria shook him hard. He suddenly snapped upright, the left corner of his mouth wet and his eyes bleary. "*Wha?*" Then his eyes focused, and he scowled. "Maria? What do you want?"

"Where is the lotus city? The one you're from?"

He groaned. "Jesus, woman, it's the middle of the night—"

"Don't call me *woman*, unless you'd like to be called *asshole*. Where is it?"

He groaned again. "In the middle of Bass Straight, east of King Island. It's the only one so close to land."

"Atlas-3, right?"

"Yes."

"How far?"

Richard shrugged again. "About 65 nautical miles south, give or take, I don't know. But they move."

Maria nodded, weighing and calculating over several long, silent moments.

"Why?" Richard asked, squinting. "What are you thinking?"

"You're going to take me out there. I want to see it."

Richard gaped at her for a few seconds, then gave a short bark of laughter. Then he frowned, as he studied Maria's face. "You're serious, aren't you?"

"Deadly serious."

"Why?"

"I have to know."

"Know what?"

Maria took a deep breath, her nostrils flaring. "I have to know the truth—that they did this to us."

"What will that accomplish?"

She spoke slowly, to calm the rising tremor in her voice. "We thought it was just terrible, dumb luck that the world ended. We blamed ourselves for failing to keep loved ones safe, food in our bellies—but really you and your lot took it from us. Took away our *right*. You and your lot signed our death warrant." Her mouth became a hateful, grim slash on her face.

"They're not my lot, that's unfair—"

"Save it. Get your clothes on. We're going."

His expression and voice both softened. "I'm not trying to shit on your loss or your grief, or whatever it is that's happened to you—" he began.

"*Grief?*" Maria gave a nasty laugh. "I'm well beyond the point of grief, my friend."

He sighed, defeated. "There's no way I'm going to be able to talk you out of this, is there?"

"Uh-uh." Maria stood there for a few moments longer, her gaze burning, her jaw clenched. "Get your shit. We roll out in ten minutes."

\*\*\*

The sky still pre-dawn dark, albeit in decline, Maria and Richard walked out the front gate towards the jetty.

Darryl was on duty again. "What are you up to?" he asked mildly.

"I need to borrow a boat. I'll be back in a little while."

"I don't think—" Darryl began, until she cut him off, drawing in close.

"Don't say anything to Vishal. This is important. You'll know why, soon enough."

He looked around, clearly conflicted. Darryl was a good little soldier and didn't like disobeying orders. "Damn it. All right. But hurry up. Make sure you're back before he wakes or else he'll tear me a new one."

"Thanks," she said gratefully, and gave him a peck on the cheek. Darryl blushed and quickly walked back to the gate.

"You know this is exactly why Vishal is throwing you, right?"

Maria flashed a tight, apologetic smile, then turned without another word.

Down on the jetty, she gestured for Richard to get into her dinghy. She unmoored it from the pier, fired up the engine and set out towards the shadow of the Reef.

# CHAPTER SIX

Maria pushed the boat to its top speed, skimming over the black water like a stone over a pond, due south as Richard directed her. He held the binoculars to his eyes, scanning the horizon.

The sea became rougher and choppier the further south they went. She had never come out this far before; probably few people had, since the Rise. Treacherous waters; frequent, violent storms. *If they were going to hide a city out at sea, this would be the place to do it.*

The horizon glowed as the first fingers of sunlight peeled back the curtain. Maria pulled down her goggles to shield them from the harsh light.

King Island appeared as a small, humped smudge

on the western horizon. Still no sign of the lotus city. "Do you think it's moved?"

Richard grimaced, shrugging. "Trust me, just keep going south. When the sun's risen a little more, you won't miss it."

Reluctantly, Maria kept on straight, but slowed down.

"Tell me more about the city," she said.

"What do you want to know?"

"How many people are aboard these lotus cities?"

"I don't know exact numbers. Atlas-3 houses about eight thousand people, at a guess. Nine, ten, if you were to squeeze."

Maria made another, more violent derisive sound. "All civilians?"

"No. There's a standing military presence. I'd say around five hundred men and women."

"Weapons?"

Richard thought for a moment. "On board or outside?"

"On board."

"Standard issue army stuff. Assault rifles, sidearms, submachine guns. No explosives though. It wouldn't do well to blow a hole in the city. It would sink faster than Atlantis."

"What about outer defences?"

Richard puffed his cheeks, thinking. "Missiles, torpedoes, .50 machine gun turrets. Covered for all types of engagements. Not that anyone's ever tried engaging before."

*Not yet.* But a brazen, impossible idea was beginning to fester in her mind.

*No,* she chided. *It's stupid. It's suicidal.*

Suddenly, Richard shouted, "There it is, coming up now. Look!"

The sun had crested in the east, spilling orange light across the water. To the south, girding the horizon, a powerful glare, like electric-white globes of plasma, cut through the early morning light. Maria snatched the binoculars from Richard to get a better look. "Oh my God," she murmured.

Richard had told the truth. She couldn't believe it. A city—a massive crystalline city, with dizzying spires and long, wide fronds projecting into the water, floating out here in the sea.

*It's breathtaking,* she thought, her hate momentarily forgotten.

"Are they going to blow us out of the water?" she asked.

"Unlikely. Torpedoes are pretty much useless for tracking small vehicles. Missiles, maybe, but they're expensive and limited. They probably wouldn't waste them on us, even if they would prefer to keep us silent. Probably banking on nobody believing us, if we talk."

*I wouldn't have, until I saw it with my own eyes,* she thought. *Wish I had my old camera.*

"Plus, there's this." Richard pulled up the sleeve of his left arm and pinched an area of skin on the underside of his arm.

Maria leaned closer, narrowing her eyes. *What is that?* She reached over and touched the skin fold, feeling something small and hard underneath, like a fat, solid grain of rice.

"An implant?"

Richard nodded. "Every citizen has one. Loaded with our personal information, clearance levels, automatic access to designated areas . . . The automated weapons systems won't attack a citizen." He gave her a wry look. "I guess they forgot to take mine out."

"That's it," she said, realisation dawning on her. "That's the proof. We don't need pictures. We just need your story, and *that.*"

"Whoa, hang on. Proof to what end?"

"Proof it exists. Proof it's worth going to war over."

"Wait, *what?*" But Maria had already gunned the engine and turned back towards the mainland, drowning out Richard's objections.

\*\*\*

"What the fuck," Jeff blurted, peering suspiciously at the lump of forearm pinched between Richard's fingers. "I can't believe it."

"Neither can I," Maria said, glancing sidelong at Richard. "But I saw it with my own two eyes."

A crowd of settlers had approached, surprised to see Maria back already, since the news of her exile had made its way around camp like a high-summer bushfire. Now they fought for a glimpse of the subdermal implant while Maria recounted what she saw at sea. They stood mystified, gaping in wonder, and anger.

"What's it like?" one of the women asked.

Maria hesitated. "It's . . . beautiful. Massive. You could fit almost all of the Bay's population in there."

"So what now?" Jeff asked, then looked past her. "Uh oh. Trouble approaching."

Maria turned to see Vishal striding towards her, arms pumping furiously.

"Vishal," she acknowledged mildly.

"I thought I told you and *Richard*," he snarled, "to get the fuck out of here by sunrise. Now I hear you took a boat, went gallivanting around the blue and then had the audacity to come back?"

"Hardly gallivanting. It was important. That thing

I told you about last night? It's true. I saw it with my own eyes. Plus we have further proof."

"I don't fucking care what you saw or what you have." Vishal's teeth were clenched, his breath ragged. "Get out. Get your stuff and get the fuck out. *Now*."

"Oh, piss off, Vishal," Jeff shouted, shoving to the front of the crowd. "You're not throwing her out after this."

Vishal cocked his head to one side, puzzlement replacing fury. "After what?"

"She told us the story. She went into the Strait and *saw it*. The lotus city. Richard showed us the citizen implant."

"Oh, come on! You're not really swallowing this bullshit, are you? And that"—he pointed at Richard's arm—"that could be anything!"

"All the same," Jeff said, unmoved, "we believe her. She stays."

"*I'm* in charge—" Vishal began.

"Because *we* voted you to lead. But frankly that leadership has been wanting lately."

Vishal looked as though he'd been slapped. "You want to vote? All right. Let's see a show of hands. All in favour of throwing Maria—this reckless, untrustworthy, manipulative woman—and this mad stranger out on their asses?"

He threw his arm in the air. A few hands at the back of the crowd went up—though their expressions didn't match the affirmation of their hands. They were afraid of him.

The smug look on his face fell like cooked meat sliding off bone, replaced by a sour grimace. "Fine," he muttered, and stormed away.

Maria turned to Jeff, gazing at him with admiration. "Check out the chutzpah on you! I am seriously impressed."

"Not that I'm not flattered," Jeff said, grinning, "but that guy's had it coming for a long time. And I bloody voted for him." He shook his head. "So now what? What do we do with this information?"

Maria pursed her lips. "I think we should take it."

"Take what?"

"The lotus city. Atlas-3."

Jeff blanched. "*Take the lotus city?* You did just say that, right?"

"You're mad," Richard whispered, eyes wide.

"Yes," Maria said, "I am mad. I'm *angry*. Jeff, you just found out those greedy pricks left you behind six years ago, and you're telling me *you're* not pissed off about it?" She turned to the people around her. "Don't you want to live again—not just survive?"

The crowd gazed back at her, stunned, shuffling

their feet and unable to speak.

"Don't you remember what it was like to eat, drink, laugh and dance—what it was like to feel happy again? I don't feel happy fighting over the scraps, do you? Why should *they* have it all?"

Jeff nodded. Soon others joined in, murmuring in agreement

"Don't you want a reckoning? A squaring of the ledger? I do. It won't get back the people we've lost, but we'll get a piece of our future back." *And vengeance,* she thought darkly.

The crowd nodded more vigorously, their murmuring rising into cries and shouts.

She turned to Jeff and laid a hand in his shoulder. "I have to see an old friend first. Then I'll tell you exactly what I'm thinking."

# CHAPTER SEVEN

As Endurance Point disappeared behind them, the sun almost at its zenith, Maria accelerated and steered the dinghy due west.

"Where are we going?" Richard asked.

"Sunny Isle."

"Where's that?"

Maria glared at him. "All that's left of the area around old Sunbury."

Richard still looked as though he had no idea where she meant.

"Forget it," she said. "You asked."

"What's in Sunny Isle?"

Maria shrugged. She wouldn't have said the

surrounding communities were friends—everybody looked out for themselves—but with the exception of the pirate bands from Raider's Bay, they had in the past enjoyed a cordial trading relationship with the other settlements. Under Vishal's leadership, however, Endurance Point had become a lot more isolationist, and suffered greatly for it.

"I still don't know what you hope to achieve," Richard said.

She was silent for a long time, watching the white spray jetting up from the side of the boat. "I already told you. *War.*"

"Do you even realise what you're saying? Do you know what you'd be throwing yourself against?"

"No. That's why you're going to help us."

"You can't be serious."

"Did I give you the impression I was joking?"

He exhaled loudly. "No. But you have to realise it's insane. Suicide."

"Any more suicidal than just waiting for our food stores and trading goods to run out?"

Richard grimaced, then shook his head. "I guess not."

"I have friends among the settlements. They'll want to know about this. Unlike Vishal, they will act. I'm sure of it."

"Even if you do manage to convince them, why would they do it? What's there to gain from this?"

It was a valid question. Why did she want this?

"We're going to capture the city, make it ours. A safe home for anyone from the coast, if they want it. Plenty of food and clean water."

"What about the people already living there?"

Her face hardened. "Why are you defending those bastards? They sent you out to sea to die, remember? *You* fought against them."

"Yes . . ." Richard replied. "Against the leaders, not the ordinary folk."

"What are you talking about, *we* are the—"

"There are good people aboard the cities. Those are the people I sought to protect by plotting against the Board—the oligarchs who dissolved the old government structures and took power on the merit of wealth and influence. Decent people, with families, children. They're not all bad."

"They took our opportunity, *our right,* to live," Maria grated, turning her head as an arc of icy sea-spray splashed over her face. "Decided we weren't good enough, by your own testimony."

"So what? You'd throw them out? Kill them? If you do that, you're no better than the people you want to depose."

Maria chose not to answer, shielding her eyes from the glare, slowing down as she negotiated the encroaching whitecaps.

Without roads and traffic, journeys across old metropolitan Melbourne had become smoother, faster; yet at the same time, the world felt a bigger place again, the crowded intimacy of old city suburban living pulled beneath the waves. Trust, the unspoken compact between strangers living in such close proximity to do no harm, to not steal or otherwise aggrieve one's neighbour, throttled and drowned beneath the water.

Fifteen minutes later, a small island appeared in the distance, rising out of the water like a single ridged plate on the back of some primordial turtle. The previous summer it had been a lush green, but the fickle heatwaves and scarcity of rainfall had seen the grassy knolls turn brown. A few large trees scattered around the isle's highest points stood watch over several concentric rings of cramped, rustic dwellings, the lowest built at least twenty metres above the waterline.

With so little land left, and even less to retreat to, the fear of the waters rising again consumed their thoughts. If Maria ever thought Endurance Point a grim, spartan place, Sunny Isle made it look like a five-star resort.

"Not much here," Richard remarked.

"They're just going day-to-day. The land's no good for farming, and they keep the highest ground empty in case they need to relocate. The Rise hit them harder than most of the communities. There's not much else for them to do, except fish, drink and hope to live another day."

"Hardly call that living," Richard said, a tinge of regret in his voice. "How will the folks here be of any help, if they're struggling so bad?" Richard asked.

Maria sighed softly. "They might not be able to help us," she admitted. "But Tāne's a good man. He knows everybody from the Marsh to East Prom. And if he has nothing to lose, and we offer him a chance for something better, maybe he'll throw in his lot with us. Maybe they all will."

She gently guided the boat along the isle's southern shore, easing off as the short, crudely made jetty came into view. Only a handful of boats remained, bobbing in the unsettled waters; most of these looked about as seaworthy as a rusty kitchen sieve. The rest would all be out in the Bay or beyond, desperate for their own miracle catch. Luckily, they had far fewer mouths to feed than Endurance Point.

She slipped the dinghy's rope around the mooring pole and pulled it tight, then they both disembarked onto the dock.

They trudged up a steep set of steps hewed into the hill rising sharply about fifty metres from the water's edge. After a short but tiring ascent, they arrived before a cluster of slipshod buildings—little more than lean-tos constructed from scrap iron and mouldering bits of wood.

"*Hull-ooo!*" Maria called out, her voice echoing among the labyrinthine metal alleyways.

"Who goes there?" a familiar voice barked sharply. Richard started as a heavy-featured Māori head popped out comically from the doorway of one of the shanties, narrowing his eyes with exaggerated suspicion. Maria clapped a hand over her mouth to keep herself from laughing.

"Maria!" Tāne bellowed as she swaggered out, beaming a huge smile. Built like a rugby player in his prime, his broad, muscular frame dominated the narrow walkway. He extended his big hands out in welcome and then wrapped his arms around Maria's shoulders, pulling her face roughly into his chest. "How you been, love?"

"Had better days," Maria said with a wry grin as he let her go.

Tāne raised his eyebrows. "Haven't we all. Come on, come in and we'll tie one on."

"It's barely even noon, Tāne."

"Yeah," he said, grinning. "But I haven't slept

yet."

Maria rolled her eyes and shook her head, then followed him into his hut.

"Who's your friend?" Tāne asked as he flopped down into an old, brown, moth-eaten couch. He reached over to the small table in front of him and unscrewed the top off a half-empty bottle of dark brown liquid, before taking a long swallow.

"Christ, Tāne," Maria said reproachfully.

"I'm Richard," Richard said, leaning forward with an outstretched hand.

"Pleasure, brother. Tāne." Tāne clasped his hand and offered him the bottle.

Richard sniffed its content, wrinkling his nose, then he took a deep swig. He quickly handed the bottle back to Tāne, coughing, his eyes watering. Tāne's laugh boomed in the small room, then he offered the bottle to Maria, who declined with a wave of her hand.

"So what's the occasion?" she asked. "Everybody else seems like they're out working."

"No occasion. Me and Kai just felt like drinking last night and didn't stop." Tāne laughed. "He's out in the blue, right now, probably hungover as shit."

*Yeah, I bet,* Maria thought. Tāne's younger brother Kai notoriously drank like a fish, but was equally well-known for not being able to handle it—unlike Tāne, who could smash a whole case of his deadly concoction without slurring a single word.

"So what brings you to our crappy little slice?"

Maria exchanged a nervous glance with Richard, biting her lip. "We've got something to tell you. Something big."

Tāne's grin died as he noticed the grave expression on her face. "Well, come on, spit it out."

"Richard isn't from around here. He's from somewhere else, out in the blue. They call it a lotus city—a floating oceanic city designed for survivors of Jagannatha . . ."

Tāne looked up, fully alert. Then he laughed.

"Come on. You're pulling my leg, aren't ya?"

Maria regarded him coolly for several silent moments.

"You're not pulling my leg."

"No," Maria said. "It's real. I didn't believe it, until I went out and saw it with my own eyes. It's real, Tāne."

"How's that even possible . . ." Tāne asked, his voice trailing off as a bewildered expression took hold. '

"They built it before the Rise, before Jagannatha. They knew about the meteor before it hit, before all this happened—and they didn't tell anyone."

"But then that means—"

"Yes." She met his gaze, letting silence speak its harrowing truth. His expression remained flat, frozen, as inscrutable as the carved faces of a Māori *pouwhenua*.

"I think you'd better tell me the whole shebang, yeah?" Tāne murmured.

Snatching the bottle of harsh home-brewed whisky from Tāne's fingers and taking a good, long swallow, Maria began to speak.

\*\*\*

By the time the story was fully told, Tāne looked decidedly less jovial, and a lot more sober, despite the bottles all being empty. But he was not angry—not as Maria had half-expected and feared. She was thankful for that, because Tāne's temper, once revealed, was a frightening thing to behold.

"That's some messed up shit, for real," Tāne said, after a morose silence.

"So you believe us?"

Tāne nodded slowly. "I trust you, Maria. You've always been straight up. Plus, you've got proof right there." He pointed at Richard's arm.

"So are you in?"

A smile broke on Tāne's face. "It's bloody crazy, but . . ." He trailed off, letting his broad smile fill the void.

"Think you can get the other communities on board?"

"We'll need numbers, that's for sure," Richard said, crossing his arms. "It'd be stupid to underestimate what we'd be up against."

"The way I see it," Tāne said, leaning forward conspiratorially, "we should try to get the support of the four major settlements: the Marsh, Kurunjang Port, East Prom and Endurance Point. Could go for Hope Hill, too, but they're a long shot."

"Yeah." Maria nodded in agreement.

"But from what you tell me, Vishal isn't likely to help you—"

"You let me worry about that," she said, a roguish gleam in her eyes.

Tāne smiled and nodded appreciatively. "All right. Well, between the Marsh, Kurunjang Port, Endurance Point and us, we'd have plenty of fuel, boats and skis, and hopefully a good number of people, God willing."

"What about East Prom?"

Tāne hesitated, taking another draught from the nearly empty whisky bottle. "They worry me. I don't think getting them over to our side will be the problem. You know why. You've heard the rumours."

She nodded. There'd always been a lot of talk, but little evidence to confirm it, and few willing to say much. East Prom was a state of secrecy, something of a localised Iron Curtain. Richard looked at them both questioningly.

"East Prom's rumoured to be a dictatorship," Maria explained. "Warragul Station, comprising of old Drouin and Warragul, stretching down to Korumburra, is the heart of East Prom. East of there are a lot of isolated settlements and flooded areas, petty colonies, and a lot of territorial fighting. Rumour is Tony Guerrero, leader of Warragul Station and *de facto* leader of East Prom, put a stop to all that." She let her words hang heavy in the air, pregnant with violent implication.

"So what does that mean, exactly?" Richard asked.

"Guerrero holds a lot of power over a large land area," said Tāne. "A lot of people, weapons *and* watercraft—but also a risky ally. Him being outside the usual circle, too, we don't know what his real motives might be. The waters are less clear."

"I'm not sure we could do it without him," said Maria, "even if, best case scenario, we got support from all the other settlements. Based on the numbers Richard gave us, we need Guerrero and East Prom on side."

"I know. And that's why I hate it. We'll never be able to fully trust them, and they'll know they have the drop on us. We need *them*, not the other way around. I don't like that hanging over our heads."

"We'll tread carefully," Maria promised.

Tāne nodded. "Okay. I'll start putting the feelers out. I'll send runners to the settlements, see if they get a nibble. If we get them on board, what then? Do we have a plan?"

"I might have something," Richard said, glancing up from his feet.

"Yeah? Care to share?" Tāne asked.

"Maybe it should wait until we've got our ducks all lined up, and then I'll share."

Tāne laughed, lifting the whisky bottle high and clapping a rough hand on Richard's back. "Looks like we're going to war," he shouted, with a wolfish howl. "Or gonna try, anyway. I think we should mark the occasion with a celebration, don't you?"

# CHAPTER EIGHT

Maria returned to Endurance Point late in the evening, her head aching. Tāne's libations—a valuable trading commodity in the Bay, and one that got tongues loose and wagging—were like scorpion venom: just a little would do. Richard groaned, laying flat on the deck like a teenager experiencing their first hangover. Maria smiled to herself.

She pulled up to the dock and nudged Richard with her toe. "Come on, we're home."

He groaned again and rose to his feet. "Never touching that stuff again."

"Don't make promises you can't keep," she

replied with a grin. "Might taste horrible and make you feel bad afterwards, but it certainly takes the edge off."

They trudged up the rocky path towards the south gate. "I never realised how hard it must have been," said Richard. "For all you guys left behind."

Maria glanced at him, scowled, then looked away. "Of course you didn't. Why would you? You had it made out there on your floating city."

"I wasn't there by choice," Richard said quietly. "But then, you think I'd refuse a chance to save my life? Would you, if the shoe was on the other foot?"

Abby and Deon's faces rose in her mind's eye. "I guess not."

"Don't misunderstand me, I'm not trying to guilt you. I understand why you're angry, why you hate them—hate *me*."

"You couldn't possibly know."

"I think I do. Why do you think I started plotting against the Board, gathering people to revolt against them?"

Maria looked at him curiously.

"Atlas-3 began as a paradise. True, the government bigwigs and the Murdochs and Rineharts still looked down on most of us. But we were safe, there was plenty of food, comfortable beds, minimal threat from the aftermath of the meteor. But things changed pretty quickly."

"What happened?"

"Within months, the wealthiest citizens began fighting with the politicians aboard, who, for once, didn't seem to have the rich's interests in mind. But money and influence can buy a lot of things—including armies. A Board of ten members was formed, comprised of the wealthiest and most powerful magnates and CEOs aboard, five men, five women. They stripped the former state officials of their power and exiled them.

"Even after that, things were okay. Life ran more smoothly. People worked to keep the city running and earned city credits, ate, and enjoyed themselves. It was business as usual, but everybody seemed eager to pull their own weight. It was no Communism, but the citizens seemed okay with that—until the Board became greedy, and began punishing the workers.

"Soon they were cutting wages, taking away their rights, lowering minimum food allowances, while they took a larger slice of everybody's action. Why they would do this, in a small, centralised economy, was beyond me: there was no need, but perhaps they had been doing it for so long, taking huge profits for the sake of it, that it was inevitable that they would do the same on Atlas-3.

Maybe they just hated us low-earning, quotidian scum.

"Over the course of five years they progressively impoverished the working citizens. Tensions ran high, and class distinction became conspicuous—parts of the city were sectioned off, the most lavish reserved for the Murdochs and Rineharts and friends of the Board. People like me, now liberated of any protection with the exile of the government ministers, and the workers, were segregated to crowded ghettoes."

"Ghettos? Really?" said Maria, eyebrow raised.

"Okay, not that Atlas-3 had any real ghettoes or run-down areas, really, but it's relative. A credit to our people, who kept our quarters clean and everything running with their own sweat and tears, even when the Board cut off funding for our sector's maintenance.

"The whole thing really deteriorated when the Board members began quarrelling among themselves. Each one had their own vision of what it meant to 'run the city', but what that really meant was which of them stood to profit the most from any given decision. A corporate war amongst our leadership, waged at the expense of citizens rich and working class alike, that tore the city apart. People were at each other's throats. The poorest stole—even killed—to get a bit of extra food for their children. I didn't think it possible that our city, which had begun as an ark, a Garden of Eden, could become so much more of the same, but it did.

"I finally had enough. I began to organise secret meetings with the workers, and we made plans to overthrow the Board. I even managed to convince a few within the Board's own military, who were dissatisfied at having become a glorified protection racket, to come to our side.

"You probably won't believe me, but while this was all happening, I did think about the people left behind on the mainland. I felt a crushing guilt. After all, we had been given paradise, and we had let it turn to ruin. I couldn't help but feel our city was, in a microcosm, what had happened on the mainland before the impact: the rich taking everything for themselves, and fuck whoever stood beneath them, or in their way."

Maria nodded, arching an eyebrow. "Ironic, huh? So what happened next?"

Richard cursed as he stumbled on a rock lodged in the path, almost losing his footing. "The day of the planned coup, one of the Board's secretaries—who himself had been treated just as shabbily as the rest of us—informed us the Board was set to meet at 10 a.m. that morning. We had it fixed so that four of our sleeper soldiers would be among the detachment stationed outside the Boardroom before it went into lockdown for the meeting. Pretty typical, you understand—they knew they'd stirred the hornet's nest on all sides, so they took precautions. We used their paranoia to our advantage.

"The plan was for our alliance's members—a good third of the city's merchants, cleaners, service staff and energy workers—to put down their kit and stream toward the armoury at exactly 10:10 a.m., giving the Board time to settle in, distracted by their own affairs. By then our sleeper cell was supposed to have subdued the armoury guards, opening it up for us to arm ourselves, in case the coup could not be handled bloodlessly. By the time we were equipped and set to march, our friends guarding the Boardroom were supposed to have disarmed and neutralised the other guards. Then we'd have a clear pathway to the Boardroom and we'd force them to surrender and abdicate. That was the plan, anyway."

"But something went wrong."

Richard nodded, his face filled with regret. "It wasn't our secretary friend or anyone within our sleeper cell who betrayed us. We simply underestimated the Board's paranoia. We didn't realise they had established years earlier a hidden network of informants and spies among the regular citizens—real Stasi-level shit. In the end, it was a gardener who brought us all down. The Board knew our entire strategy."

"So it all fell apart."

Richard shrugged, sighing. "Our sleeper soldiers never even got to open the armoury. We were all arrested on our way there. A phony trial by kangaroo court, and then the executions began. Every man, woman or child associated with our alliance, killed by hanging or firing squad."

"They—executed everybody? Even the *children?*"

"Every single one. Anyone who had even a slightly dubious connection to us, too. Made the whole city watch."

"Why?"

"To set an example for the others, to keep the rest from stepping out of line."

Maria froze, facing him, her upper lip curled. Her voice came out as a hoarse, savage whisper. "But *why the children?*"

Richard's eyes glowed with hate, his face twisted at the memory. "Didn't want any seeds left in the earth to grow into sedition, one day, I guess." Then his hatred dulled, and his face became slack with guilt. "Only the other leaders and I were spared execution. They had a worse punishment for us.

"We were beaten, tortured within an inch of our lives, then taken out in boats until the fuel tank ran dry, then left without food or water to die slowly under the hot sun. Two boats would go out, only one went back. Our punishment wasn't the slow death, the Board told us at sentencing, but living with the knowledge that our treachery had led to the deaths of an entire third of the city." His eyes glistened with angry, withheld tears. "They were right. That was worse than dying."

"Fucking monsters wearing designer suits," Maria growled, as they reached the gate. She nodded to Darryl, who returned the gesture. The bonfire was roaring again, casting a warming glow across the dark camp. "Surely they had to realise by killing so many people that they only made their position that much more unstable?"

"Did they?" Richard asked, pausing mid-stride. "Didn't you ever read Machiavelli? It's better to be feared than to be loved. Fear *commands* respect and obedience where love only requests it. By showing their willingness, the ease with which they could sacrifice a whole third of Atlas-3's population, they made their position that much stronger. No one will stand against them."

"Would the citizens stand with us?" Maria asked. "If we make it aboard, and they're as oppressed as you say, would they fight with us?"

"I don't know." Richard pursed his lips. "People often stick with the devil they know, no matter how terrible."

"What about if they see you? Would you inspire them to join us?"

Richard scoffed. "If anything, seeing me would probably send them running for the hills. They saw how well it went with me last time."

"Maybe you can be something more than just a dreadful reminder. A symbol for something more."

"What might that be?"

"Unity—the end of class and wealth divisions. People united by common humanity, common survival and mutual benefit."

Richard thought on this for a moment. He nodded his head slowly, warming to the idea. "Maybe. Maybe. We'll just have to wait and see if anyone is crazy enough to join with us."

"Don't underestimate Tāne. He's got a silver tongue, and people tend to like him. If anyone can convince them, he's the guy."

They sat down on a log by the bonfire, staring solemnly into the rippling flames. Embers tumbled high into the air. The heavens wheeled overhead, whorls of dazzling white pinpoints spangled upon crushed velvet night. Maria couldn't remember seeing so many stars in the city, before the Rise.

Jeff had pulled out his guitar and was riffing on the other side of the fire, and singing—badly. A group of boys and girls kicked a battered, slightly deflated football around, laughing and yelling, clouds of dirty dust stirring around their ankles.

"So what's your story?" Richard asked.

Maria shrugged. "Spent the first two years out in the wilds with my kids, fending for ourselves."

"You've got kids?"

Maria slowly shook her head, not looking away from the fire. "Not anymore."

"I'm sorry."

"It's okay." It wasn't really, but what else was there to say?

"Their dad still alive?" He nodded towards the wedding band on her left hand.

Maria averted her gaze, focusing on the children wrestling over the football. "He didn't make it out of the city. He was working in the CBD when that first tsunami came flooding in."

Richard looked at his feet, shaking his head. "It's not fair, is it?"

"A mother should never have to say goodbye to her children."

"Are you . . ." Richard hesitated. "Are you starting this war because of the people? Or because you want revenge?"

Maria sneered. "Why can't it be both?"

"Because personal vendettas pollute the virtue of our cause."

"There wouldn't be a need for the cause if those bastards hadn't left us all behind," she snarled, rising to her feet and leaving Richard alone by the fire.

# CHAPTER NINE

Heavily armed outriders swooped in on Maria's vessel, one on either side, as she and Richard made their final approach towards Kurunjang Port. The boat on the starboard side drew in close, the patrolman behind the gun mounted on the gunwale lowering his mirrored aviator shades and regarding them suspiciously. He wore nothing from the waist up except a Kevlar vest; his bronze arms were pocked with scars. The boat on portside waited, machinegun aimed at their hull. Then the patrolman nodded to the gunner in the other boat and streaked away without a word.

Richard's face had turned a bloodless white.

"What the fuck was that?"

"Kurunjang's water police," Maria explained. "They're the reason Kurunjang Port is the safest place in the Bay. Even the pirates think twice, now."

"I can see why."

Maria pushed the boat forward. Soon, the port rose up to greet them. Maria slowed down, gliding into an empty slip between a faded fishing trawler the colour of bleached seagrass, and a white-and-blue deck boat in slightly better condition. She tied the boat to the moorings and helped Richard up onto the dock.

The wharf didn't look as busy as it sometimes did—half the slips were empty, and the oceanic traffic cops, as she came to think of them, were absent. Only a handful of wharf workers and crewmen moved on the docks, unloading shipments, descaling fish, or otherwise standing around smoking.

"Think this is going to work?" Richard asked.

"I damn well hope so," Maria said. "But Eva Jacobs is going to be a tough sell." *Hell, they all are,* she thought. *Life out here might be a pile of crap, hard and unforgiving, but people have gotten used to it ... Almost made peace with it. Are they really going to want to disrupt their lives for a promise I'm not even sure I can deliver?*

"You're asking people to offer their lives, maybe

even die. It's no small thing."

They moved away from the docks towards the rear of the wharf. The port looked different to the other old-world ports—although weathered and bleached by both sun and salt-water, the dock was relatively clean and new, lacking the slime and decrepitude of tide-ravaged wood. Patches of iridescent fish-scales shimmered in the bright light, baked onto the sealed gum planks. Thin stretched colonies of barnacles rode the pilings.

Because this had once been a residential district, there were no warehouses—instead, the whole back of the wharf was an open-air agora filled with bamboo and wooden stalls and colourful sun-sails. Sweet and savoury smells, sizzling meat and grilled fish permeated the air. The stalls were manned by merchants and tradespeople, bartering their wares from sunrise to sunset. A person could get almost anything here, most of the time: guns, ammo, *meat*—the thought of a medium-rare steak, like in the old days, set Maria's mouth watering. A person could buy a hot meal, drink themselves stupid on something that tasted like turpentine, get into a fight, maybe even hire the company of a pretty warm-bodied woman for a couple of hours, and forget their problems for a short while.

Yet today, some of the stalls stood empty, and

fewer people than usual travelled among them. The traders seemed grizzled and belligerent, even when someone stopped and gave their goods a long hard look, especially the food-sellers—almost as if they didn't want to part with their offerings. *This is why I'm doing this,* Maria reminded herself. *If we can take the lotus city, no one in the Bay will be hungry again.*

"Do you think your plan will really work?" she asked.

"I really don't know," Richard replied earnestly. "The implant keeps the defences from targeting an individual. Whether or not it'll protect a whole fleet, or even part of a fleet around me—well, that remains to be seen."

"Let's focus on getting that fleet first, I suppose."

"To answer your question, though—I'm optimistic."

Maria gave him a rueful smile. "That'd be a first."

"I'd be stupid to rush into another conflict," Richard replied thoughtfully. "I was optimistic once before, too, and we were routed, nonetheless. We planned the whole thing meticulously. Optimism isn't about commitment or zeal. It's weighing up the sum of one's experience and observations."

"So what makes you optimistic this time?"

Richard smiled. "They didn't shoot us out of the water that first time we went out to see it."

A shiver inexplicably ran down the length of Maria's body, like a long chill breath blowing on the nape of her neck.

"I can't believe how different this place is," Richard said, marvelling at the people around him.

"Kurunjang Port is lucky," she said. "They've got access to the sea, but there's still grazing land not far out of town, land that hasn't been too badly hurt by the droughts or salination. They can raise cattle and grow fresh vegetables—though both are in dwindling supply and very expensive. They also control the major trading routes inland, meaning they've got their choice of trading partners at any given time. They don't have to sell for less to scavs like us."

Richard made an apologetic face, then looked away.

The centre of the agora was filled with delectable aromas, foods Maria hadn't tasted for a long time: grilled beef cubes, spiced pork, bird meat stuffed with peppers in hot flatbreads—more likely seagull or pigeon than chicken. They sidled up to a meat vendor and Maria haggled for a beef skewer with red peppers and onions, offering the vendor twelve .22 bullets for two skewers.

The vendor shook his head vigorously, his unshaven jowls quivering.

Frowning, Maria reached into her jeans pocket and pulled out a crumpled Ziplock bag of weed. "What about this?"

The vendor squinted, scrutinising the hairy buds, scowling. Eventually, he grunted and said, "I suppose I can trade it for something else," before handing her the skewers.

"Trading marijuana for meat. I've seen it all now."

"It's a hardy plant and has a lot of uses—though most people do just smoke it. They've got a lot of worries—something to take the edge off. Especially if they can't handle Tāne's homebrew swill."

Richard grinned and tore a hunk of beef off the skewer. He chewed laboriously, savouring the flavour. "Man, that's good."

"I'd kill for a real steak," Maria said. "I'm so sick of fish."

"I haven't had fresh meat in years," Richard said. "All we had was fish, or canned or dried—" He stopped, his cheeks reddening. "Oh. Shit. Sorry."

Maria sighed, relenting. "No. Go on."

"The lotus cities have almost everything: gardens

and domed greenhouses the like of which haven't been seen since the Hanging Gardens of Babylon, irrigated by a complex networks of canals with desalinated water; vast stores of cured meats; massive deep-freeze vaults of poultry to last up to ten years. You wouldn't believe how much canned, dried and non-perishable food they have aboard. Not to mention all the seafood the city's dragnets pull in. I mean, for fuck's sake, the city has *restaurants*—can you believe that?" He hesitated again, averting his gaze, then cleared his throat. "But fresh meat—livestock, fresh chickens—there's just no way for a lotus city to sustain them. Too much space needed, grass, et cetera, stuff that's just not possible or viable at sea. The frozen meat is still good, but it's just not the same."

Maria raised an eyebrow as he lapsed into silence, walking on in silence.

"Jeez, I'm sorry. I shouldn't—"

"It's fine," she said. "You're just telling me the truth."

"I'm sure it doesn't make it suck any less, rubbing it in."

"Well, you'd be right on that front."

Maria strolled back towards the docks and hunkered down by a guano-splattered piling, looking out over the sea.

"For what it's worth," Richard said, "I really am sorry."

"For what?"

"For everything that's happened. To you, and everybody else."

Maria took a deep breath and exhaled slowly. "You don't have to apologise. I keep directing my anger at you, like you're a symbol for that place. But you fought against them, the Board. Maybe once you were a cog in the machine, however ignorant. But not anymore. I think I'm the one who owes you an apology."

Richard gave a small smile. "It's okay. We're good?"

Maria smiled back, nodding. "Yeah, we're good."

"If we do win, there will be unity and peace for us all," he said, meeting her eyes with disarming sincerity. "I promise you that."

"Don't promise something you're not sure you can deliver," she said, shaking her head. "People are stupid. They'll always find something new to fight about."

"Don't be so cynical. Under the right conditions—"

A boy of eight or nine years old suddenly came dashing up to them. His hair was dirty, unwashed, clammy with sweat; he wore tattered cut-off jeans and a miserably faded orange T-shirt with a half-peeled shark decal. "Ms Maria?" the boy asked.

"Yeah?"

"Miss Jacobs sent me. She's waiting for you up in her office." The boy nodded his head up the weathered old tar road behind him, its surface scarred with potholes and deep channels. "Come on. I'll take you to her."

Maria and Richard rose to their feet and followed the boy out of the agora.

***

Despite her diminutive form and youthful appearance, it was clear why Eva Jacobs ran Kurunjang Port. Dressed in a black tank top and leather pants banded with metal studs, her hair half-shaved and pushed to one side, and thick kohl rimming her piercing azure eyes, Eva cut an intimidating figure. She looked no older than twenty-five, but her presence radiated authority and commanded respect. Her wrists tinkled with metal bangles of various colours extending halfway up her forearm, in similar fashion to the Bay's pirates. Maria found herself wondering whether Eva had once belonged to the pirates—either as a raider herself, or as a one-time concubine. Rumour was they pillaged for flesh and carnality as much as food, weaponry and boats.

"So," Eva began, her eyes evaluating Maria, "you want to attack a settlement no-one has heard of before, somewhere out in the blue."

"Yes," Maria said.

Eva shook her head, exhaling noisily. "I don't know, Maria. War is expensive—especially on the human front. It's not good for business. Not good for families already struggling if they lose a mum or a dad."

"*Business*," Maria repeated, grimacing as if she'd eaten something unpalatably sour. "God, I hate that word. The men and women aboard the lotus city had their mind on business, too—business as usual. And look what it cost. What it cost *us*."

"People are adapting. The world has changed, but so have we. You want to send them to war, reminding them of everything they lost? For something they might not even win?"

"If we work together, Eva, we *can* win."

"Do you really believe that? We have peace, for the most part. Life is hard, but there's *peace*."

"For how long?" Maria demanded. "How long do you think peace will last when the food starts running out, and people start getting hungry? When the clean water is in short supply and people are fighting just for a sip that won't make them sick? The drought's punishing the land—soon cattle will be untenable. The soil's producing less and less—that's why your merchants charge an arm and a leg for a few stunted veggies. We have to go further and further afield for fish, because the water's either polluted or overfished in the immediate area."

"Maria, you don't know what's going to happen. The rain could come any day now—the lands could become green again, the cattle could start breeding, the crops could start growing—"

"And if it doesn't? What then?" Maria leaned forward, hands clasped before her.

"Think about it," Richard said, chiming in for the first time. "You could all have a home, a place that's safe, where food and clean water is plentiful. A life that's *better* than all this. All the people in the Bay could be afforded this. But to take the prize, we've got to risk big. Risk it all."

Eva laughed silently, shaking her head in disbelief. "That's easy for you to say. You have nothing to lose. You just want to go home."

Richard glared at her defiantly, mouth curled.

"Richard is a good man," Maria interjected. "He

fought against the Board—Atlas-3's leadership—to make things better for the people. He has nothing because he risked everything for the hope of a better world."

Eva's mouth twisted as she chewed the inside of her cheek, her eyes searching. "There's more to it than that, though, isn't there?"

"What do you mean?" Maria asked.

"For *you,* Maria, I mean."

"Does it matter?"

"Yes. If we're going to be partners, all our cards need to be on the table."

Maria's expression hardened, her chin jutting out. "All right. It's about getting justice. An eye for an eye. Those rich pricks took away our future. It's time for us to take away theirs."

"Revenge, then?"

Maria said nothing.

"And that's worth throwing lives down the gauntlet?" Eva demanded. "Didn't you ever see *The Count of Monte Cristo?*"

"You don't think it's worth it? Aren't you just a little angry, learning all this? And what about your people—how will *they* feel, once they know the truth? All those people killed, probably a great many of those deaths preventable. Did you lose anyone in the aftermath of Jagannatha that could've been saved, if we'd been given the chance to board the lotus cities?"

Eva looked away. Suddenly she seemed a girl of fifteen, hiding behind punkish makeup and clothes and a tough demeanour, her face drawn, wounded. "It doesn't matter anymore," she murmured.

"Yes," Maria said. "It does. If you and your family—like mine, like so many others still alive today struggling in the Bay—had been given the chance to board, they'd still be here."

"There's no assurance of that."

"No, you're right. But we'd have all had a fighting chance. My kids might not have died from hunger or preventable disease. You might not have had to grow up so fast."

Eva flashed her a searing look, incensed by the assumption, but then her face softened.

"And now," said Maria, "maybe we can make life better for those left behind."

"Do you have a plan?" Eva asked.

"We do," Richard answered. "We'll have a better idea though, once we know who's on board. The whole thing comes down to our numbers."

"And who else has declared their allegiance?"

"Right now . . ." Maria sighed. "Just Endurance Point and Sunny Isle."

Eva's eyes widened, and she looked as if she might laugh for a moment, but she didn't. Her face became serious again. "Your war could be over before it even begins."

"We're working on it," Maria said.

"You'd better," Eva scowled. "I don't want Kurunjang footing the entire cost all by itself."

Maria lifted her head. "So you'll join us?"

Eva nodded. "Kurunjang Port is with you."

Maria smiled, extending her arm. "Thank you."

Eva clasped Maria's arm, sealing their pact. "So what now?"

"We're waiting on Tāne and a few of his runners to come back from the other settlements. Should hear back tonight or tomorrow."

"Did you send someone to Warragul Station?"

"As a matter of fact, yes," Maria replied.

Eva's expression darkened. "Be careful with Tony and East Prom. Been hearing a lot of disturbing rumours lately. Expanding territory and whatnot. He's not to be trusted."

"We'll be careful," Maria said.

# CHAPTER TEN

The following night, Tāne arrived at Endurance Point. He was grinning from ear to ear as he strode into camp. A couple of kids, Hakan and Sabrina, came to fetch Maria.

"Tell me you've got good news?" Maria said, striding up to greet him.

"I would have come yesterday, but one of my runners got held up in the Marsh."

"Right."

"So how did you go with Kurunjang?"

Maria smiled. "Eva's on board."

"That's good, that's good."

"So? You gonna leave me in suspense?"

"Cal from the Marsh is in. Not so lucky with Dorian up at Hope Hill, though."

"Well, they were always a long shot." Hope Hill didn't really have a stake in the affairs of Hidden Bay, anyway. They didn't trade or involve themselves with the other communities unless absolutely necessary. "And you, how did you go with Tony?"

Tāne's face tightened, apprehensive. "That's the bad news. Ariki and I went and spoke to a guy named Westfield—representative of Tony's. No go."

"Shit," Maria muttered. "Why?"

"Apparently his forces are committed elsewhere—a bunch of colonies I'd never heard of. Said something about a cannibal problem." Tāne gave a crooked smile. "Cannibals! Can you imagine that?"

"Sounds like the rumours are true then. Guerrero's playing regional policeman."

"Seems that way. But doesn't help us with our problem."

Maria sighed. "How many people is Cal committing?"

"Nothing in stone yet. But I wouldn't get your hopes up."

Maria nodded. The Marsh was a small place with

a large population. The old Bacchus Marsh area had flooded badly during the Rise, turning it into a fetid quagmire, but the populace had largely survived, and adapted—building a labyrinthine colony of stilted homes and walkways above the swamps. The trouble was about a third—or maybe more—of their population were elderly, infirm, or young children. With fewer able bodies to provide food for the settlement, the Marsh risked more lives than simply those joining the war effort.

"Even with my guys and yours, based on the numbers Richard said we'd need..." Tāne said, frowning.

"We really need East Prom on side." Maria pursed her lips, hands planted on her hips. "Crap."

"Yeah."

Maria exhaled, dragging a hand down her face. She felt beaten before she'd even charged out of the gate.

But the stubborn, angry voice inside quickly overshadowed her encroaching doubt. *No. You're not giving up on this. We can't give up so quickly. They cannot win again.*

"What're you thinking, mama?" Tāne asked.

"Richard and I will go to East Prom tomorrow and talk to Guerrero ourselves."

"I was just there. Trust me—"

"I don't mean any offence, Tāne. I do trust you. There's no one I would trust more than you on something like this. But maybe this one requires a different strategy."

"What do you mean?"

"We need Richard. A man like Guerrero will only join us if he thinks there's something in it for him. Instead of appealing to his humanity, we appeal to his greed. Richard might be able to offer him something nobody else can."

"Do we really want Guerrero having that kind of advantage, though?"

Maria threw her hands up, flummoxed. "He already does. What else can we do?"

\*\*\*

A bank of clouds rolled in from the east, momentarily obscuring the hot sun. *Seems fitting,* Maria thought. The tension was palpably thick, an unmistakeable sense of foreboding as they made their way south-east towards East Prom. Maria noticed it in the long silences, the averted eyes of her friends.

She wondered if they had noticed the stillness, the lack of boats on the water, too.

Maria banked and followed the coastline east. She was in unfamiliar territory now. East Prom began a new namesake promontory, like a shepherd's crook pointing south at its tip and spreading east into old Gippsland. Warragul Station itself, where they were heading, was the eastern half of old Drouin merged with Warragul, extending all the way past Ellinbank.

Apparently, the existence of such a large settlement—the largest in the whole Bay—was necessary, and justifiable: it was home to tens of thousands of people, many of whom, rumour had it, had fled from further east in the years after Jagannatha. Great forests had turned to salty marshes; and, when it wasn't sopping wet, the bush grew dry and sparked at the smallest tinder.

Guerrero told Tāne on his first visit that the petty settlements beyond the furthest borders of East Prom constantly engaged in skirmishes with their neighbours, even daring occasionally to infringe on East Prom's sovereignty. And when times were especially lean, some even engaged in cannibalism. That's what Guerrero *told* him.

"He looks like a shark," Tāne had remarked, recounting the meeting to Maria. "A great big fuck-off white pointer. Cannibals. *Pffft. He* looks like he'd just as soon eat you as look at you."

As the journey continued, large buildings began to appear on the shore, flanked by tall, snaking cobblestone walls that stretched for kilometres along the coastline. The tin roofs showed signs of corrosion, evidence of patch-jobs over the years. In six years, the risen seas had already begun to erode the land, creating cragged cliff-faces of soil and exposed roots and slipshod overhangs that one day would succumb to the sea. *This must be old Drouin*, Maria thought. That meant the port, down in the southern part of old Warragul, was not far off.

The walls grew higher as they drew closer to port; soon tightly curled razor wire adorned their heights, guarded by tall wooden watchtowers fixed with mounted machine guns. And still there were no boats out on the water.

"It looks like a prison camp," Maria murmured.

"I was thinking the same thing," Richard said.

"Think you can handle this, Richard?" Maria asked.

Richard nodded. "I've dealt with worse men than Guerrero before. Even if he is all he's rumoured to be."

"Good."

The first thing Maria noticed, when the docks

finally swam into view, was the sheer number of soldiers guarding the port: heavily armed with assault weapons, shotguns and sidearms; bedecked in plain black uniforms with black boots, Kevlar vests and helmets. Her guess was that either Guerrero, or someone preceding him, was ex-military. There was no way to explain the weapons and kit they had otherwise.

There were few boats moored along the docks. A fishing trawler not far from the slip where Maria tethered her boat was in the process of unloading large nets of silvery fish. As the crew hauled the catch up onto the dock, overseen by a single soldier, Maria noticed the fishermen were wearing matching yellow uniforms. Maybe that was the reason they hadn't seen any ships along the coast—they were heading far into the blue to get big catches; moreover, it looked as though fishing—boating in general—was tightly regulated and monitored.

Two soldiers carrying large guns guarded the mesh gate between the docks and the settlement proper. Maria and Richard disembarked and approached cautiously, noting the hard glares of the soldiers in their direction.

"Name?" one of the soldiers asked.

"Maria Beaumont. Richard Campbell."

The soldier bent down and picked up a clipboard

from the plastic chair nestled against the fence, frowning. "Maria Beaumont, Endurance Point?"

"Yeah?"

"I'm sorry, your entry into the town has been denied."

Maria's face twisted into a scowl. "Why?"

"You've no goods to trade, and you haven't got permission to wander around the town unescorted. Frivolous visits are strictly prohibited."

"This isn't a frivolous visit," she growled, before checking herself. "We've got to speak to Tony Guerrero. And why am I on a no-entry list—"

"Mr Guerrero doesn't just see any riff-raff—" the other soldier began.

The first soldier coughed, shutting his comrade down mid-sentence. Evidently the more diplomatic and professional of the two, he said, "Mr Guerrero is unavailable at present. If it's urgent, you can speak to his advisor, Aaron Westfield, and he will pass along anything you have to say."

"Tāne already spoke to Westfield yesterday," Maria protested.

The soldier looked vaguely amused. "Well. Then you have your answer."

"We really must see Mr Guerrero."

Both soldiers subtly angled the muzzles of their firearms towards them. Richard stepped back, grabbing Maria by the shoulder. "I think this was a mistake," he said.

Maria shook his hand off, glaring over her shoulder, then she met the first soldier's grey eyes. "Fine. You tell Westfield—"

"—that Richard Campbell from Atlas-3 wishes to see him," Richard interrupted, "to discuss a proposition."

"What the fuck is Atlas-3?" the soldier grunted suspiciously.

"What proposition?" the other soldier demanded.

"A proposition to help him expand his territory," Richard replied.

\*\*\*

The short walk from the port to the main settlement was enough to confirm Maria's impression of East Prom: there were even more soldiers in the streets, almost one for every two or three citizens. And these were no green men dumped into their role: these were hard, practised, fighting men, even before the Rise. Ex-military, almost certainly.

Citizens pushed rough-hewed wooden carts through the streets, transporting firewood, apples, grey piles of descaled fish. Others toiled over steaming buckets of bitumen, patching holes and ruts in the asphalt, or manned stalls handing out provisions to queues of people. A shabbily dressed few watched them from the beneath the old awnings, smoking cigarettes, unabashed in their open, hostile regard. Most, however, stole only furtive, fearful glances, never quite meeting their eyes.

A small girl with lank brown hair and a ratty, oversized cardigan outside the old supermarket met Maria's eyes, then placed a pale finger over her lips. A soldier near the door spotted the girl and grabbed her brusquely by armpit, cursing, dragging her into the building, out of sight. Maria's skin crawled.

*This is a bad idea,* she chided herself, fearing for the girl. Too late to turn back now.

The soldiers from the pier escorted them down the main street, stopping outside a squat building with large tinted windows—a solicitor's office, at one time or another. Two more soldiers stood guard outside. One of the guards, a big surly man with an ugly scar slicing diagonally from nose to the right corner of his lip, nursing an M4 carbine, nodded to their escort wordlessly.

The escort turned around and headed back in the direction they came.

"Through there," the scarred solder grated, nodding towards the door. "Ten minutes."

"Is Mr Guerrero in there?" Richard asked.

The guard glowered at him. They slipped inside without another word.

A slender man with slicked-back dirty blond hair, wearing a fine black high-collared suit and a crooked smile, awaited them in the foyer. "You must be Richard. And Maria, was it?"

"Westfield," Maria said curtly.

"We don't have much time, I'm sorry to say. Mr Guerrero—"

"Is he here?" Richard blurted.

Westfield smiled. "Yes, he's here. He was most interested in your . . . proposition."

Maria glanced at Richard hopefully. *That's a promising start.*

"This way, please," Westfield said, gesturing down the hallway.

Maria and Richard began to move, but Westfield abruptly halted them.

"Not you. Just Richard."

Richard met Maria's eyes, his expression at once

nervous, but determined. "I'll be fine."

"Please step outside until the meeting is over," Westfield instructed. "I will come and get you afterwards."

Begrudgingly, Maria exited the building.

\*\*\*

Tāne was right. Tony Guerrero *did* look like a shark.

They were ushered back into the foyer about twenty minutes later. That Guerrero had given Richard more than the promised ten minutes seemed a good sign—moreso, when Guerrero and Richard both emerged from the office smiling.

Guerrero looked as though he'd just swum around in a cloud of chum.

"Hi," he said, extending his hand to Maria, "I'm Tony. Good to meet you."

"Likewise," she said. She tried to sound warmer than she felt. "So, where do we stand?"

"Consider us allies," Guerrero said proudly, clapping Richard on the shoulder. "Richard has convinced me taking Atlas-3 is the right thing to do."

Maria sighed with relief. "It is," she agreed. "When this is done, there'll be enough food to go around, clean water, and space for people to live."

Guerrero frowned at that last one. "And a mobile launching point," he added, his tone buoyant.

Maria looked at him questioningly, but he didn't elaborate.

"Anyway, you go and draw up your plans," Guerrero told Richard, leaning in close, "then send word when we're ready to assemble, okay?"

"You got it," Richard said.

Guerrero clapped his shoulder again, grinning, then turned back to his office. "See you on the battlefield."

Maria shot Richard a damning look as Westfield escorted them out. *Richard, what did you do?*

\*\*\*

They returned to the port in silence, not speaking until they were back on the boat, with East Prom vanishing behind them, and no eavesdropping soldiers.

"What the hell did you promise him?" Maria demanded. "Mobile launching point—what does that even mean?"

Richard glanced at the deck, his face taut. "A strategic point at sea," he said, hesitating, "from which he could deploy his forces."

Maria's eyes widened. *That's why Richard baited him with expansion of territory,* she realised. *It's the only thing Richard could have given him.*

Nevertheless, she was fuming.

"That was not part of the plan," she growled.

"I know."

"You had no right to offer him that!"

"This was your idea, alright? I convinced him; I just took it a bit further. I had to. He wouldn't have gone for it otherwise." Richard rubbed his face. "I was lying anyway."

"Tony Guerrero doesn't know that." She wrestled with the steering wheel and angled the boat into the trough of an oncoming wave, cresting, spraying foam as the bow crashed into the water on the other side. "Nor would he care. You've given Guerrero license on behalf of all of us to come and invade our communities, take anything he wants. You overstepped the line. No, you blew it out of the water."

"Listen, I got him on-side; we needed him for his numbers, and now we've got them—two hundred soldiers, plus an additional two hundred conscripts if needed."

"Conscripts," she repeated, frowning. *Whatever*

*the hell that means.* "Two hundred people still isn't enough. We can't rely on an extra two hundred *maybes*. Christ, Richard, you basically sold him the whole Bay for peanuts and a promise."

"Look, let's just worry about taking Atlas-3 for now, and we'll cross the Guerrero bridge when we come to it, all right?"

Maria turned away in disgust, staring out over the grey horizon, growing blacker as the thunderheads gathered. An ominous portent, indeed.

# CHAPTER ELEVEN

"I've been thinking about our numbers problem," Tāne said, as they sat around the fire at Endurance Point, Natalia and Jeff now joining them. "I think I might have a solution."

They waited in suspense. He seemed hesitant.

"Well, go on, spit it out," Maria said.

"You're not going to like it."

"Can't be any worse than the Guerrero thing, can it?"

Tāne almost choked laughing, before he became serious again. "No, it can get worse."

"Okay," she said, cautious. "Let's hear it."

"Between Kurunjang Port, East Prom, the Marsh, Sunny Isle and here, we've managed to get four hundred people—tentatively six, with Guerrero's so-called *conscripts*. But that's not going to help us in the initial assault. That's a good start, but not nearly enough, right, Rich?"

"I think we're going to need a solid six hundred, to even stand a small chance. More, if we can, but no less."

"But *how?*" Maria asked. "Where else can we go?"

Tāne raised a finger. "There is one place, but like I said, you're not going to like it."

They all waited with bated breath.

"The pirates."

"*What?*" Maria, Jeff and Natalia balked in unison.

"You've gotta be out of your fucking mind, Tāne!" Jeff shouted, face awash with disbelief.

"Now hang on," Tāne started, a rueful, appeasing expression writ upon his face. "Hear me out. They've got the numbers—and we wouldn't need all of them, just the bare minimum to fill our armada. Let's say a hundred."

"A hundred murdering, raping bastards," Maria muttered.

"They've got more guns, ammo, fuel and fast watercraft than all of our communities combined. And yes, they *are* murdering, raping, thieving sonsofbitches, and plenty else. But they were hit by Jagannatha and the Rise and everything that's come since, just like us. And they weren't always murderers and thieves. They're just playing the cards they've been dealt, like the rest of us.

"But if we offer them a stake in the prize, offer them a seat at the table, maybe they, and we, can put all the bad blood and bad history behind us. I'm not suggesting for a minute we can ever trust them. But the enemy of my enemy is my friend, right?"

"I didn't think it could get worse than Guerrero," Maria said, shaking her head. "But hell, you really know how to throw a firecracker on the birthday cake, Tāne."

"I don't like it, either, mama, but I don't see a lot of choice."

Maria searched the firelit faces of her comrades and grimaced. She hated it, but if they were going to have a fighting chance, she knew he was right.

\*\*\*

"This is stupid," Tāne said as he guided the old, beaten speedboat into the narrow inlet.

"It was your idea," Maria reminded him.

He shook his head reproachfully, perhaps chiding

his own foolishness.

A thick snarl of clouds slid across the moon's bright face, deepening the gloom. Tāne slowed to a crawl as the canal narrowed and the ramshackle walls of the fortress—cobbled together from the harvested parts of ship hulls and gutted factories—began to enclose them, a rusting, haphazard canopy of metal spikes, exposed rebar and sharp hull plates.

Raiders Bay. Maria had only heard rumours—no-one had come so close to the pirates' fortress and lived to tell of it—but its sharp, cruel scavengers' aesthetic matched the fear and dread inspired by those nebulous tales. If Vlad the Impaler had survived to the modern era, and survived the Rise to make himself a home, this is probably what it would have looked like.

A comparison well deserved, Maria saw, as they passed the first rotted corpse, impaled on a sharpened metal spear from anus to mouth.

"What are we doing?" she murmured. "How did I ever let you talk us into this?"

"These guys make Tony look like Santa Claus," Richard said, barely a whisper.

As the twisted canopy blocked out the starry sky, they soon spotted the threshold—and it was open. The pirates of Raiders Bay had no need of a door, for they had no fear of trespassers.

Maria's hands were trembling, her teeth quietly chattering from an internal chill.

The boat slid across the gaping threshold and into a lagoon shored up with high rusting walls, festooned with shabby wood-and-metal platforms and walkways forming a labyrinthine network between small clusters of shacks and lean-tos. The vault of the sky opened up once more, like the roof of a sporting arena in the summertime—only this arena was filled with water, and looked more like something out of *Mad Max*. The pirates' fleet stretched in a horseshoe from one side to another, moored to the struts of the wall, packed so tightly that one could hop from boat to boat. The sound of drunken laughter rang clear and savage across the still night.

A loud engine groaned to life, and a spotlight on the far side of the lagoon blinked sleepily for a few moments as the generator powered up. The beam swung around and fell upon Tāne's boat, near blinding them.

A loud crackle cut across the raucous background noise, before an amplified voice chortled, "You silly fucks. You know where you are? Are you lost?" A pause. "Don't worry about that, pets. We'd be pleased to come down and make your acquaintance. Sit tight, now."

"This is bad," Tāne said, his hand slowly

dropping for the old F1 submachine gun sitting in the alcove near his feet. Richard's expression had gone from nervous to terrified.

"Don't be stupid!" Maria hissed. Tāne withdrew his hand as if scalded.

Maria raised her arms in the air, half-blind from the spotlight. Richard did the same. There was no telling what was happening out on the shadowy platforms; for all she knew, every gun in the place could be trained on them. *But they haven't used them yet*, Maria thought, daring herself to hope. *They haven't shot us dead. Maybe they're curious.*

A jet ski zipped across the black lagoon, carrying two passengers, stopping along the boat's port side. One of the riders, a foul-smelling man with hair the coloured of burnt toffee, dismounted and climbed over the gunwale, flashing a grotesque, uneven, yellow-and-brown smile.

"Chuck your guns to me, nice and slow like, then move back and sit down. That one, too," he said, pointing at Tāne's F1. Maria and Richard removed their handguns and kicked them across the deck. Tāne handed the submachine gun over to the pirate with an unhappy look on his face. The pirate, on the other hand, looked like he'd just fallen in love.

"Step aside," he instructed Tāne, taking over the steering wheel. The vessel pivoted starboard, thrusting towards the moored vessels along the righthand side of the horseshoe. The pirate guided it along the curve, before killing the engine and sliding to a stop beneath an overhanging rope ladder.

"Up you get, then. You lot first. Don' worry, I'll take good care of your boat." The pirate grinned.

One by one, Maria and her crew ascended the ladder. The platform above was teeming with pungent, grimy raiders, clad in tattered, rotting shirts or none at all; black spiked leather vests and chaps, as if they'd pillaged a sex shop warehouse. Chains criss-crossed unwashed skin reeking of salt and sour alcohol; rotted jeans above blackened feet. The crowd jeered and catcalled, a few trying to grab Maria as she passed. She shrank away from the groping hands, hugging the rickety railing as she walked.

There were few women, but the ones they did cross had collars around their neck, held tight by chains clenched in men's fists. Filthy, dejected faces framed hollow eyes, gazing absently. Maria felt her anger rising, surging up her throat like acid, but she willed herself to remain calm. Nothing good would come out of her losing her cool.

At best they'd kill her quickly. *At worst* . . . she thought, glancing back at the chained women.

They were escorted into a large hall at the end of the walkway. Orange light flickered from makeshift braziers scattered across the room. Human skulls clotted the eaves inside and out. At a long, rough-hewn table sat three men in leather jerkins, talking quietly amongst themselves, and two collared women, naked from the waist up. The men were bearded, muscular in a way that was more pragmatic and slab-like than showy and sculpted. They continued eating and drinking without pause, heedless to the unruly jeering and howling that now flooded the hall.

The two women—one brunette, the other with hair the colour and sheen of volcanic glass—stared at Maria with heavy-lidded, seductive eyes. The black-haired woman's tongue touched the corner of her lips and stayed there. Maria felt herself redden, stifling her discomfort.

The men at the table soon lifted their heads, as if noticing the newcomers for the first time. They stared in silence for several tense heartbeats, their faces inscrutable.

Finally, the one in the middle spoke—a man with short-cropped, sandy-brown hair and a spade-shaped goatee. The cacophony around them died as he spoke, a silencing flicker within the hive's consciousness. "Do you have a death-wish?" he asked quietly. His voice was calm, even dignified.

Nobody answered.

"Brandt asked you a question," growled the pirate sitting to his left—a thick man with a shining scalp and large, square beard. "You'd best answer."

"Do you have a death wish?" Brandt repeated.

"No." Maria's voice rang strong and loud, betraying none of the fear she sheltered inside.

"What you say and what you do don't line up."

"We have a proposal for you. A peace offering."

The pirate on the right, closest to the black-haired woman, regarded her salaciously. Maria suddenly felt naked, and dirty. Black-haired, hatchet-faced, with a pink, puckered bullet scar on his left cheek, like a tiny asshole, just above the corner of his mouth, exposing teeth. "Maybe she wishes to join the harem?" he said.

"The first one who touches me loses it," Maria snapped, eliciting laughter from the pirates.

"She's not one for the harem, Patersall," Brandt said, his tone icy. The laughter died instantly. "Too much fire. She's right, she'd cut your dick off and feed it to you. So keep it in your pants."

Patersall glared at Brandt, remaining silent.

"Who are you?" Brandt asked them.

"I'm Maria of Endurance Point. Tāne of Sunny Isle," she said, pointing, "and Richard from Atlas-3."

If the pirates were curious about that last one, they didn't show it. "A proposal, huh?"

"A chance for a better life, one where you don't need to do *this* anymore."

More laughter.

"We've discovered something, something shocking," Maria continued. "The government and the wealthy escaped the mainland before the Rise started, even before the meteor."

"We know."

Maria gazed at them in confusion. "Know what?"

"About the exodus," Patersall said. "Of course, we didn't find out until much later."

"*You knew?*"

"Oh yes." A furtive smile crossed Brandt's lips. "We know about the floating cities out in the blue."

Maria continued staring, agog, before her mien darkened. "Then you know why we're here."

"I can guess. You've just learned about the city's existence—which I presume is called Atlas-3, where your friend Richard here comes from—and you want to try and capture it? Am I right so far?"

"So far."

Patersall and the other pirate smirked.

"And you assume we hadn't already thought of that ourselves?" Brandt asked.

"Had you?"

He sneered. "Of course. Only after we got a taste of their arsenal we realised it was suicide. My thought is you know that, too—you thought you could persuade us into joining you, dangling the city like a carrot before the horse, then use us as cannon fodder. Petty revenge for all the years we've harassed you, while *you* and yours take the prize. Why else would you come here?"

"We came to make *peace*," Maria insisted, sensing the encroaching danger, the menacing postures of the savage men surrounding them. "We came because we are desperate, and we need you. We need you to help us set this injustice right, and take back what belongs to *all of us*, together."

"How noble. But I find it a little hard to swallow." Brandt nodded to his men. Strong arms seized Maria, jerking her wrists behind her back. Tāne and Richard shouted and struggled as the pirates swarmed them.

"What are you doing?" Maria demanded.

"You came with your proposition, and we

listened." Brandt's face darkened. "And we say no." He nodded towards the far door. "Take them to the plank and shoot them in the fucking head."

The pirates began hauling Maria and her friends across the hall, out onto the opposite walkway.

"*No!*" she cried, then a callused hand cracked across her face. Her mouth flooded with salty, metallic warmth.

"Shut your mouth, bitch!" a rough voice from her periphery commanded.

Maria spat blood in her assailant's face, struggling to break free of the restraining arms. "You're making a mistake!"

"You made the mistake, coming here, thinking you could deceive us."

Beside her, Tāne broke free and took several of the pirates down with fists like oak clubs, a bloody-knuckled Maori warrior of old baring his teeth and flaring his nostrils—until a grizzled, scarred raider with a milky left eye clobbered him across the jaw with a wooden cudgel, sending Tāne sprawling on his belly.

Richard's struggle died as Tāne went down, his body limp, his face crushed with hopelessness.

Maria jammed her heels into the doorframe, pushing back hard. The two pirates hauling her pushed and grabbed, straining, then a third came to help; her legs began to shake but she didn't give. Finally, a fourth pirate—the same one that clubbed Tāne—swept up and skull-thumped her with the club. Her legs turned to water and the human tide carried her out onto the walkway.

"No . . ." she moaned, the word leaking from her mouth like a rope of drool.

She staggered along the walkway, escorted brusquely by two reeking pirates, struggling to stay conscious—the world faded in and out, black to grey to black again, her heartbeat pounding in her ears. They crossed a rope bridge to a dizzyingly high platform, buttressed against the fortress wall and hanging precipitously over the dark lagoon.

*A plank*, Maria thought, her mind reeling. They were going to be walking the plank. *Dropping off into black eternity.*

They really were going to die.

She was forced to her knees. Maria had never felt a gun against her head before. It was cold, hard, yet sickeningly inviting; a doorway she wasn't yet ready to cross, but which beckoned her nonetheless. She saw, in her mind's eye, Abby and Deon and Luke, standing at the threshold, ushering her towards them.

*Let it go,* her mind whispered. *Go to them. End your*

*pain.*

Beside her, Tāne looked down into the frothing black abyss, his face wet, the colour drained. Richard, tearless, was stooped over in dejected silence, defeated.

Brandt, Patersall and the other pirate stood on a balcony above their great hall, while the other pirates crowded the walkways, bridges and platforms in rapt silence, practically salivating.

Their executioners stood ready, waiting for the signal.

*We're going to die,* Maria despaired, *because they think it's suicide. They think we wanted to throw them into the meat grinder.*

*No,* another voice whispered. *You have the chip. The implant in Richard's arm.*

The light switched on.

"*Wait!*" she cried. "Don't kill us! We have a way past their defences! A chip!"

"Fucking shut it, bitch!" the pirate behind her snarled, nudging the muzzle against her skull.

"Wait," Brandt's voice pealed out across the fortress. "What chip?"

"*Show them,*" Maria whispered to Richard.

Richard slowly raised his left arm into the air.

"I see an arm."

"The chip is inside the arm, implanted," she cried. "It keeps the defences from targeting the owner, and anyone close to them. It'll help us get in."

Brandt remained silent for a moment, ruminating.

"Okay, new plan," he said. "Cut his arm off, then *we* can go take the city."

"It won't work without me," Richard said. "The chip is linked to my vitals, my heartbeat. If I die, or I'm not attached to it, access is cut off. You need me alive. And whole."

Patersall scowled. "We should fucking kill them. Fuck the city. We don't need it."

Brandt's face twisted, his jaw clenched, as though in pain. "Release them," he said hesitantly.

"What?" one of the executioners cried.

"I said *let them go*."

"Brandt—" Patersall started.

"I want that city. And that dick is going to get us inside."

"What about my friends?" Richard demanded.

"Unnecessary," Brandt answered.

"Then I'll throw myself into the lake and drown," he said, hobbling on his knees, inches shy of the platform's edge. "Then you'll get nothing."

"Fine," Brandt snapped, turning on his heel, waving a hand over his shoulder.

The would-be executioners hoisted them to their feet, nudging them back towards the bridge. Maria's heart beat wildly in her chest.

Back inside the hall, the leaders sat down once more at their table with their concubines, as Maria, Tāne and Richard were pushed down into the free chairs around the table. Maria scowled at Patersall next to her, who gazed at her hungrily.

"So," said Brandt, nonchalant, as though he were hosting a family dinner, "tell me your plan, and more about this floating city."

# CHAPTER TWELVE

The swell rose and fell like the failing breath of titans. The seagulls hovering curiously over Maria and her flotilla seemed louder for the deathly silence that had taken over.

Maybe this was natural before a battle—the calm before the inevitable storm. She had no idea. This was so far outside her experience. A graveyard chill rippled through her, like a portent.

*What am I doing?* she thought, dwarfed by the immensity and viciousness of the thing she had set in motion. *I'm in over my head. All these people, my friends—they could die today, because of me.*

The harder voice inside interjected: *We fight because we need to set this wrong right. To stop people from continuing to suffer, no matter the cost. We can't run from this.*

"You all good?" Richard asked over her shoulder, riding double on her jet ski.

"Just nerves. I'll be fine."

The lotus city loomed on the horizon, a diamond glimmering on the water.

"Reckon they know we're here?" she asked.

Richard made an amused sound. "They picked us up ages ago. We're a huge blip on the radar. My ID would've registered with Central."

"So they know you're coming back." Maria took a deep breath, releasing it slowly, willing the butterflies in her stomach to be still. "You ready?"

Richard nodded against her back.

Maria spun the handle on the old air alarm siren fixed to the front of her jet ski. The sound was taken up by boats spread out among the flotilla, signalling for the gunboats and hit-and-run outriders to begin their advance.

The vanguard split into two wings, one veering left, the other right. The speedboats and jet skis rode at the head of the pack, while the gunboats cruised a little behind. Maria and the rest of the boarding party—

primarily riding jet skis and a few fast boats—watched from a distance. She gazed through the binoculars with trepidation, waiting for the battle to be begin.

Eva and Westfield rode at the head of the left van, slicing towards the shining city. The missile salvos and the machine gun turrets were turning on their platforms, tracking them. The right van sped forward, a spear of rippling black flags with a smattering of other colours. The pirate fleet rode hard and fast, outriders and gunships alike, their vehicles modified for maximum speed, agility and fear tactics. Brandt's flagship, a Black Bullet yacht fitted with several machine guns and extra shield-plates around the gunwales, led the pack. Cal, the dreadlocked leader from the Marsh, and his small band rode scattered amongst the horde, a brief flash of colour in a sea of screaming black brigands.

The first rocket from the floating city streaked into the air, belching yellow-grey smog. Eva and Westfield split apart, yawing in opposite directions. The boats and skis scrambled. The rocket struck a boat at the rear of the pack, sending a blast of water and shredded boards flying into the air.

The battle's first casualty.

The sea erupted with the thunder of automatic weapons. The pirates' gunboats fired a steady salvo, the machine guns spitting out bucketloads of hot lead. The jet skis swerved and skimmed over choppy, frothing seas, misdirecting the city's targets. Blood-crazed pirates laughed and screamed as they fell, pitched into the water or dismembered by .50 gun turrets.

Suddenly, Maria spotted one of the pirates aboard Brandt's ship pull out a rocket launcher, hefting it onto his shoulder. *A fucking rocket launcher!* "Damn idiots are going to blow a hole in the wall, sink the damn thing!"

"Bloody hell," Richard said, watching in horror. "We have to stop them."

The .50 machine turrets hacked through the water like a blind chef, carving through boat hulls, chewing up decks, smashing riders into the sea in a bloody ruin. The missiles screamed into the sky at widely spaced intervals, catching the attackers whenever they strayed too close together.

And now explosions began to detonate from beneath the water, capsizing boats, shattering keels and hulls, throwing jet skis in close proximity into the air. Torpedoes had joined the deadly assault.

The pirates were being mowed down, but they kept on fearlessly, riding hard and fast, screaming with utter abandon, unbreakable.

The left van was faring poorer. Maria couldn't

make head nor tail of what was happening, or who had fallen, or whether Eva or Westfield were still alive. All had descended into foaming white and red chaos.

So many dead already. The city's weapons seemed inexhaustible. Every explosion felt like a seam tearing in her heart, stitching being plucked one thread at a time.

"We can't just sit here," Maria grated. "We have to help them."

"No. We have to wait until we hear the sirens and the flares go up."

"*They're getting slaughtered out there!*" Maria raged.

"We *have* to wait for the signals."

"We don't even know if the signal carriers are still alive!"

"Maria, don't do anything stupid. We have to get aboard that city."

Maria hyperventilated, watching the chaos and explosions across the water. *No.* She couldn't watch anymore. She couldn't wait. She had to—

"We have to help them."

"Maria, *no!*"

Maria's hand flew to the crank of the air siren fixed to her handlebars and a doomsday alarm squalled out across the flotilla.

"What are you doing—"

"Shut up," Maria snapped, before shouting as loud as she could: "Move forward, boarding party! Close formation, weapons hot!"

The jet ski surged forward, skimming over the ocean like a stone. The rest of the group sped up behind her.

The gleaming city pierced out of the water, scratching the clear sky. Reflected sunlight burned like hot stars across the sharp spires. The roar of machine gun fire and thrumming motors, the crumpling of wood and metal, was deafening.

"*No!*" Richard cried, his voice nearly lost in the cacophony. "*You'll kill us all!*"

The bubble-domed turrets, like death-spitting pustules, turned towards their advancing spearhead. Jet skis flipped, oily black smoke boiled into the air. Boats floundered, or crashed into their neighbours. The formation began to disintegrate.

*The plan's not working,* Maria realised with dawning horror as they drew closer to the city. *The weapons platforms are still targeting us—Richard's implant isn't working!*

"*Scatter!*" she tried to scream, but she couldn't even hear her own voice in the din. All was screams and chaos and madness: death reaping a grand harvest.

Maria's skin tingled, warming despite the terrible shiver down her back. The air on her left side felt hot, superheated. Then a shrill, tortured scream pierced the howling madness.

She turned and saw a man on a small gunboat behind her rippling with flames, his skin blackening, shrieking and clawing at his face.

A woman on a jet ski east of him burst into flames, a flailing, screaming human torch.

*What is happening?*

"We need to board," she whispered dully, though no one could hear her. The sound was bleeding out of the world; she felt faraway, detached, a marionette tugged to and fro in the battle's rhythms. She darted around a massive piece of floating hull and sped towards the lotus city's southern frond—the place where she was supposed to board with the others, from which they would launch their invasion. "We need to board *now* and shut down those platforms."

"Maria, look out!"

Richard's voice jerked her out of her trance, moments before the turret found her, hard geysers spitting seawater like chips of concrete. She turned hard, hair-pinning, almost crashing into another ski. The turret cut the other ski down in a red mist. She sped away from the city, panic seizing her.

Fires were burning everywhere now; boats burned, spewing smoke into the cloudless sky, while bodies continued to spontaneously combust around the battlefield.

*What is happening, what is happening—*

She and Richard should be dead.

She spotted Jeff, riding toward her on a black and green ski, his face wrought with terror. He fell backwards at a sickening angle as a .50 slug tore through his chest, liquefying flesh, organs and bone, jettisoning red ruin.

*"No!"* she moaned, her heart snapping in half. *No, no, no—Jeff!*

A missile soared overhead and dipped, plunging into a speedboat gliding up along the centre. The explosion threw fibreglass and steel, a dismembered arm, across the beleaguered flotilla. A larger, ragged piece of steel sliced like a buzz saw through the air and sheered one passenger's head in a nearby boat clean in half. The sea was a roiling maelstrom of confusion.

*It's over*, Maria thought dismally. *We're finished.*

Another explosion, bursting to her left. All sound disappeared as if in a vacuum.

Something hard struck her across the head. She whipped forward against the handlebars, smashing her brow. As the world went dark, the thighs around her waist loosened and slipped away.

\*\*\*

*It's snowing*, she thought drunkenly, as her eyes fluttered open. Powdery, light grey snow, falling in a fine mist across the water.

She pushed herself upright, gazing about at the carnage.

*Not snow. Ash.*

Fires burning upon oily, bloody water. Bodies smoking like industrial stacks in the saddle, raining crematory ash.

The place that would be their home, in all their wildest and now murdered dreams, had become a charnel house.

*Rout. Total rout.*

The explosions had slowed down, become irregular, but the guns and screams still perforated the funereal silence. This would ever be a cursed place, she thought, her mind reeling.

The sea, a graveyard. Cursed, it had been, cursed from the start. A mass Viking funeral, a glade of derelict pyres for fallen warriors for whom none would sing dirges and cry laments. There was almost no one left.

*Rout. Total rout.*

The siren, long and mournful in the smoke and ash, woke the survivors from their stupor. A consolidated sound, the engines, roaring away, fleeing. There was no honour here among the dead, just a sense of waste and hopelessness.

It was all for nothing. Jeff. Richard. God knew who else. Gone.

The siren faded in the distance. The guns had fallen silent, the weapon platforms still. They had drunk their fill of blood.

*Retreat, retreat.*

Maria pushed herself upright, almost falling off her seat, her head spinning. Her hand tightened around the throttle, and she followed the doomsday siren out of the ashen gloom. The sun fell upon her back once more, pregnant with false hope.

# CHAPTER THIRTEEN

She didn't remember limping back into port, nor remember shutting herself away. The pain of her concussion, the pangs in her stomach, those who came and went, none of it registered. The sorrow—which stank of charcoal and ash and clung to her skin, a miasma permeating her every fibre—had leached all consciousness from her, all memory, all hope.

There was nothing left. There had been no greater good. She had started a war born of hate and loss.

They had died because of her rashness. Her friends, her allies, people depending on her, had died for a false promise. They had died for *her* vengeance.

She should have died with the rest.

She wanted to cry, but the well was empty.

Tāne came and sat by her bed. She was sure he was a ghost, but he spoke in a tangible low murmur, a soul weighed down, and she felt his hand, warm and conciliatory, upon her back. He was still alive, at least. But the revelation came with no joy. She felt incapable of ever feeling joy again.

She should have listened to Richard when he said to wait. In her ignorance and fury, she had brought nothing but destruction to her friends and allies.

Time became like water sliding through fingers. Eventually her hunger pangs grew so bad, like daggers, forcing her to rise and stumble out, dazed, a body sapped by depression, clawing for something to cease the pain.

*There is one way.*

Maria made her way up the stairs, away from the shacks and up towards the outlook, the picnic area. *Sunny Isle.* Tāne was up there, along with Eva, Natalia, and Westfield, who had his right arm in a sling and a deep cut across his face.

Everybody sat close together, united in hopelessness and grief. Even the few remaining pirates joined them, their smug grins wiped away, their swagger concussed from their bodies. Neither Brandt, Patersall nor the other lieutenant were present.

Tāne spotted Maria at the head of the stairs and came over. His arms and forehead were spotted with yellow and purple bruises. Eva came to join them.

"Any food going?" Maria whispered.

"I can get some, if you like," said Tāne.

She gave a weak nod, avoiding his eyes. "How many?"

"What?"

"How many, Tāne?" her voice croaked. "How many came back?"

He let out a long sigh. "No more than a third."

She was wrong. The well wasn't fully dry.

Tāne closed his arms around her shoulders, squeezing her tight. "It's okay, it's okay," he whispered. But he was wrong—it wasn't okay at all.

"It wasn't your fault, Maria," Eva said, laying a comforting hand on her back.

"I rushed in there. I led them to their deaths. Goddamnit, Richard told me to stay the course, but I didn't listen—"

"If you'd stayed, more people would have died."

"That's just it. More people died anyway. Richard's plan didn't work. The tracker failed. I led my group in to help, and—" She couldn't even say it. The tears burned like hellfire on her cheeks. "I started this, this whole stupid fucking crusade. I got them all killed. Richard, Jeff . . ."

"You started it for a good reason," Tāne said. "You wanted to end the famine, give us all a second chance. This isn't life—what kind of life were we living before this? Sooner or later, time was going to run out. You saw the writing on the wall and decided to act. You inspired us, gave us hope again."

"No," Maria snapped, her face twisting in self-loathing. "I did it for myself. I did this because they took my kids, my husband away. But even that's not the truth: Jagannatha, the tsunamis, the Rise—they took my family from me, and ever since I've been looking for someone to blame.

"When Richard came along and told me that story, and I saw the city with my own eyes, I was just… *so angry*. I wanted to lash out and scream. I wanted them to bleed and suffer, so *they* knew what it was like to lose."

Eva's hand came flying up, stinging across Maria's cheek. At first she thought it was out of anger, until she saw Eva's tormented, perplexed eyes.

"*Get a hold of yourself*," she whispered savagely. "We all chose to be here. We all knew the risks before we signed up. We knew what it might cost. There's nothing to be gained in blaming yourself here. We all had personal motives for coming. Mine's not so different from yours." Her mouth curled in fury. "We trusted you to be our leader in this thing. With Richard gone, you really are our last hope. So wake the hell up and stop feeling goddamn sorry for yourself, and *come up with a new plan*."

"You—you still want to do this?" Maria asked, wiping her face.

"We've got nothing left to lose," Tāne said.

"We have to get back on our feet and try again—make a new plan," Eva said, jutting her chin. "We can't let our friends' deaths be in vain."

"You're right," Maria said, nodding, wiping her face. "We can't let it be for nothing. We need to come up with a new strategy—"

"The plan was flawed from the beginning," Westfield interrupted, joining them. "The chip was never going to guard anyone except Richard himself."

"He's dead, Westfield. Obviously, it didn't work for him, either."

Westfield made a sour face. "One of many things he left out. I'm particularly incensed that he didn't mention the lasers during our planning."

"Lasers?" Maria scowled in bewilderment. "What lasers?"

"The people spontaneously combusting? Military grade laser weapon—able to generate high enough wattage to light a human being up like a candle. Something Richard never told us about."

"Maybe he didn't know."

"Or maybe he left it out."

"Why would he do that?"

"That's a very good question. Why indeed?"

"In any case, if we're going to give this one more try, we need to play it smarter. Quieter."

"How would we do that without Richard's chip to get inside?" Eva asked.

Maria sighed again. "I don't know. There's so much we don't know about the city layout. Richard never really gave us much idea of the terrain or plan once we were inside." *Another thing he left out.* Maybe he wasn't banking on their success. "How many people do we have left, exactly?"

"Just under two hundred, though a proper count hasn't been done," Tāne answered.

"Can we call in back-up now?" Maria asked Westfield.

"Mr Guerrero is unlikely to deliver any additional forces," he said, shaking his head. "Not after the severity of our losses. I am probably not welcome back at Warragul Station." Beneath his cool, professional facade, Maria saw traces of unhappiness ebbing through the cracks.

Maria looked over at the few remaining pirates. "Anyone?"

One with a shaved head and tattoos climbing from his neck to his scalp spoke up. "Brandt is dead, so are Patersall and Vasquez. Saw their ship go down with my own eyes. As it stands, they brought us *all* in. There's no reserves. Whoever is left is right here."

"I might be able to get a few more," Eva said, hesitant, "but honestly, after our spectacular failure, it's going to be a tough sell."

Maria rubbed her eyes. "You sure you still want to do this? Because it's not looking good."

"The odds for winning are still better than those given for Jagannatha hitting us," Tāne said, grinning slightly. "So I'm weirdly okay with our odds."

The survivors nodded in agreement.

"Okay," Maria said. "As far as I see it, we don't have any idea of ventilation layouts or access from the outside. We don't have advanced cutting tools so there's no getting through windows or walls—none of that *Mission Impossible* stuff. That basically leaves the original plan: access via the quay."

"We saw how well that worked last time," Westfield sniffed.

"That's because we went bashing on the front door. We need to sneak past their defences this time."

"And how to you propose we do that?"

"Well, before I get to that, there's one more element I need to lay out." Maria took a deep breath. "You're not gonna like it."

"Spit it out," Tāne said.

"We need to wait until the seas are rough and there's a storm brewing."

"*Out in the Strait*?!" Tāne blanched. "Did you whack your head out there on the water?"

"Richard said the radar works on two bands—one is really sensitive and doesn't work well in bad weather; the other can cope but isn't as accurate. I'm taking that to mean it won't pick up small targets."

"Not the jet skis again," Westfield groaned.

"No," Maria said. "We *dive*."

"*What*?"

"We dive. Snorkel, scuba, whatever. We wet-suit up, we dunk in the water a few clicks out, and we swim to the quay."

"Out in the Strait," Tāne deadpanned, "in the middle of a storm."

"Yes."

"You're nuts."

"They won't be expecting it. Anyone here not a strong swimmer?"

Nobody put their hand up.

"We'll need a distraction, though. This time, not a bunch of fast-riding skis. In fact, the opposite. Someone out there, literally holding up a white flag, hoping they'll notice."

"They're not going to fall for that!" Westfield protested.

"We don't need them to. We're not expecting them to open the gate for a parlay. We just need to keep them distracted. The boats getting our swimmers out there will come up on radar. If, however, once we're swimming, there's a boat holding up the white flag, it might divert attention. Plus with all the debris from the battle floating around out there, it'll be easier for them to write off."

"A lot of assumptions there, mama," Tāne murmured.

The group mulled over the idea. A few began nodding their heads.

"And what if they decide to attack?" Westfield asked. "Who's going to volunteer for the white-flag suicide mission?"

Nobody answered straight away. Then, after a brief murmured exchange with his comrades, the shaved-headed pirate raised his hand and said, "We'll do it."

"You?" Maria asked. "Why?"

"We've got even less to lose than the rest of you. And . . ." He hesitated. "We've done a lot of terrible things these past few years—things that I can't even say. Doing this . . . it's a small step to rebalancing the books, in my mind."

Maria nodded. "Thank you."

"What's the plan once we're inside?" Tāne asked, his voice hopeful.

"Let's keep it simple: we swim for the docks, hopefully undetected, while our flag-wavers keep the city's eyes on them" *And hopefully don't get blown out of the water.* "Then we slowly make our way through the city. We've got two objectives, and, I'm afraid, without knowing the lay of the land, neither is going to be easy. One is to neutralise Central Security, cut off their communications; the other is securing the Board members, forcing their surrender. If we do this right, we'll have the element of surprise, unlike Richard's first coup, and we can catch them with their pants down. If we lock down Central Security first, we'll have eyes around the whole city, then we can move into phase two—getting the Board members."

"Resistance is going to be fierce," Westfield said. "They're going to have the advantage."

"Hopefully the element of surprise, and familiarising ourselves with the terrain before they realise we're there, will shift the odds in our favour."

"What about the rest of the populace?" Eva asked. "We can't expect them to just roll out the welcome mat. They're going to want to defend their home. What do we do with them, afterwards?"

"I've been thinking about that. Once this is done, if we actually manage to pull it off . . . We extend the olive branch, make peace."

Heads shot up, wearing puzzled, distressed expressions.

"There's already been too much death," Maria said. "The way Richard described it, the citizens have no love for the Board or their totalitarian regime. Once we liberate them of that"—*supposing we don't die*—"we show them we can be better. We extend the olive branch and open the city up to the people of the Bay and Atlas-3 alike. Open it up to the idea of unity." *It's what Abby and Deon would have wanted.*

A grin slowly stretched on Tāne's lips. "I like it. It's crazy as fuck, but I like it. Let's do it."

# CHAPTER FOURTEEN

The spearhead of boats slowed as the swell became choppier, and the sunset became a bruise in the west. There was already almost no distinction between sea and sky. They would be crossing an abyss closing in on them from all angles.

Every eye on the crowded decks was locked south, but there seemed little hope of spotting Atlas-3. Without Richard to guide her, Maria had been relying on the assumption that the city, lit up from within at night, would be like a ghostly lighthouse out on the tempest. But that assumption seemed to be wrong, and no such lights appeared out on the black horizon. Perhaps the city was able to mask their interior lights somehow.

And now, as the whitecaps were becoming more numerous, slapping violently against the side of the boat, fast-moving thunderheads piling against the field of stars above, Maria was becoming desperate.

"Maria," said Eva, pointing out over the water. "There's the graveyard."

*Yes.* Maria fought the ache in her heart that threatened to buckle her resolve again. *The graveyard.* Moonlight glimmered along bullet-pocked jet skis and shiny bits of jetsam floating on the water's surface. Much of the stuff that hadn't sunk straight to the bottom had likely been carried away by the currents, but a large concentration of debris still remained. She hoped it meant the lotus city wasn't far.

Scanning from left to right, Maria caught a glint of dull silver a little further south of the wreckage. *Atlas-3.*

"Got it," Maria said, pointing.

"That's a bloody long swim," Tāne said gravely. "Five or six kilometres, at least."

*Even worse with guns strapped to our backs.* "Anyone who doesn't think they can make it, it's now or never. Last chance to back out." Maria waited for someone to speak up, but nobody did.

Maria nodded, satisfied. "You ready to go?" she asked Tāne and Eva.

"Not as ready as I was a few hours ago," Tāne replied.

"All right." She smiled nervously to the rest of her crew. "This is it. Stay close—tight formation. Keep an eye out for each other. We can't afford to lose anyone. Let's go."

Maria jumped into the water, and nearly screamed. Even in her wetsuit, the chill pierced her flesh like a thousand icy daggers.

The others climbed over the bow and gunwales and dropped into the water. Startled cries went up all around, limbs peddling to keep the warmth flowing. Plugging their mouths with a motley of standard dive regulators, full-faced rebreathers and plastic snorkel tubes, the last fighters of the Bay began their long, freezing swim.

The sun's last rays bled away into total night. Maria's small army swam in total unnerving blackness, broken only by the fickle whorls of starlight above. The sea grew rougher, tussling and pulling the swimmers, dunking them relentlessly. Before they'd even covered a third of the distance, Maria's arms were burning with exhaustion. The lower half of her body felt heavy, her cold-numbed legs like stone pillars. Thankfully, her crew were pushing back against the sea—they did not flag nor give up, driving through fatigue and futility. Even when the first rumble of thunder pealed above them, the first purple flash of lightning lit up the sky, they did not falter.

Atlas-3 rose out of the sea before them like a ghostly glass temple, glazed purple and blue by branches of lightning, looming impressively as its needle-like towers scratched the vault of heaven. They were almost there. She could hardly believe it, but it wasn't over yet. Any moment now, those .50 guns could come online and chew them all into shark bait.

Forcing the fear from her mind, she drove her arms like spears into the water, pulling harder, in-out, in-out, one-two, one-two . . . The guns remained silent and still.

Maria swam at the tip of their formation, guiding them towards the long, narrow silvery frond cutting out onto the water, bobbing in the mounting swell.

The mouth the quay was a large, open L-shaped portal along the tip; big enough to accommodate small- to medium-sized vessels. Maria swam towards the tip, stretching the formation out into a line. Under the curved glass-and-steel latticed roofing, dozens of boats were moored along a steel pier—all sleek, black and red carbon fibre, like the one she found Richard in. She grabbed hold of the moorings, pulling herself half out of the water, gasping but overcome with gratitude. *We made it! We actually fucking made it!*

Just then, a mountainous swell rose beneath them, causing many of the swimmers to smack into the quay, crying out in pain.

Those at the rear were not as lucky. The massive wave broke upon them like a great watery fist, pulling them beneath the frothing surface. After several breathless moments, a host of heads broke the surface, spluttering, floundering in panic.

A few, however, did not resurface.

Tāne, who'd popped out of the water beside her, looked as though he was going to dive back in and attempt a rescue. She grabbed him by the arm and said, "Don't be stupid! I want to help them too, but we can't—not out in this."

Grimacing in reluctance, he nodded.

Much to her surprise, the quay, as far as she could see, was empty. No guards.

She and Tāne helped the rest up onto the deck. One by one, the tired swimmers clambered up the pilings and support struts, dripping and shivering.

"How many did we lose?" Maria whispered to

Tāne, once the last person was out of the water.

"I don't know. Twelve?"

"Damn. Where's Eva?"

"Right here," came a tired voice behind Tāne. She wore a wry grin on her face, already shaking water from her weapon, inspecting. They crouched down to steady themselves as the pier jerked up and down, left and right, with the sea's undulations.

"Everybody check your weapons. Let me know when you're ready to move."

Maria kept expecting a siren to sound or soldiers to start streaming down the quay at any moment, but nothing happened.

"Ready," Tāne said. Eva and Westfield both gave the thumbs-up.

Maria nodded. "Let's do this."

The wetsuit-clad invaders swept up along the decking, moving quickly but quietly. She wanted to get out of the quay before any shooting started. If they were intercepted now, it'd be a massacre; all the ducks lined up in a neat row, with nowhere to go.

The frond swayed and bent with the swell, articulated at regular intervals to allow the fronds to cope with rough seas. It really was a remarkable design. That it could take the impact of a tsunami without toppling, according to Richard, without smashing the quays clean off the main structure, was incredible, especially those first massive ones surging up from the ebbing wound Jagannatha had slashed into the South Pole . . .

An airlock waited at the end of the dock. It didn't require a key, passcode or chip scan—there was just a single green button secured behind a Perspex casing, itself securing by a circular latch mechanism.

Maria turned the latch, lifted the case and pressed the green button. The airlock's outer door snapped open, hissing loudly.

"I'll lead the first group in and check it out. Tāne, you're with me. You guys wait until I signal you the all-clear."

Eva and Westfield both nodded. Maria, Tāne and half the boarding party crammed into the airlock and pushed the red button on the other side of the wall. The clear doors snapped shut like crocodile jaws, the hiss louder with the storm muffled outside. Maria pressed the green button on the other side and the internal door slid open. Tightening her grip on her MP5 submachine gun, Maria led them slowly into what appeared to be an atrium.

The atrium was bathed in warm, golden light radiating from thousands of thin, dangling whorls of luminescent icicles. Marble floors of white, black, and violet, chased with occasional swirls of red; mezzanines and terraces and walkways reaching out in every direction, criss-crossing on either side of the atrium. Shops, restaurants . . . all the things from the old world they'd lost.

A massive staircase rose from the atrium floor to a mezzanine area, then a second, more opulent level. A large structure, like a skybox in a sporting arena, dominated the upper level. Two exquisite golden statues stood looking over the atrium, a pained expression wrought on the face of a powerful form bent beneath a monstrous globe.

Maria recognised it immediately: the Titan Atlas, bearing the weight of the world upon his shoulders as punishment for warring against the Olympian gods. A perfect symbol for the lotus cities—the last bastions of civilisation, bearing the weight and responsibility of humanity's survival upon themselves.

A task they had failed abysmally, Maria thought.

Every one of the intruders stood drinking in the sights, eyes like dinner plates, their jaws hanging open in amazement, their hatred and purpose almost forgotten. It was everything they could have hoped for, and more.

It was beautiful and magnificent—but something

was wrong.

*This is too easy. It's too . . .*

*Too* empty.

The small flaws in the glamour did not reveal themselves immediately, but when they did, it was hard to imagine how she had ever missed them. They weren't small at all—something major had gone down.

The city was eerily silent, except for the occasional electrical crackle emitting from the hallway to the right. Sparking light fixtures created a strobing effect in the corridor threshold. The shutters on the restaurants and shops were pulled down, the signage lights dull and grey. Broken glass and ceramics and spent bullet casings littered the floor. A smaller alabaster rendition of the same statue of Atlas lay toppled, split clean in half, the Titan's back broken by the weight of his charge.

The red on the floor wasn't part of the marble, but congealed blood.

*What happened here?*

And still no sign of the city's denizens.

"I don't like this," Maria murmured, circling around. "Go and get the others," she instructed the woman next to her. The woman ran off towards the airlock.

"Shit, look out!" a man cried, pointing upwards.

Maria's gaze shot upwards up, following her comrade's finger. Helmeted, black-garbed soldiers crowded the walkways, long, squarish weapons trained on them. The sound of running boots and short, sharp shouts surged up along the corridors.

They were surrounded.

Those uniforms ... Maria squinted. Some of them bore a pyramidion logo that, read vertically, bore the insignia *A3—Atlas-3*. But the others ... their uniforms were almost identical, though plain, without insignia. Still, the resemblance, the familiarity, was uncanny.

*No ... Can't be.* Maria remembered with dawning horror where she'd seen them before. *It's just not possible—*

They looked exactly like East Prom soldiers.

The others filed in from the quay, their arms raised in surrender. Westfield and several wet-suited men followed behind them, guns drawn.

"Westfield ... What the hell's going on?"

"Sorry, Maria," he said. "Nothing personal."

A loud, unified springing sound, like the twang of a hundred crossbows at once. Something hard and sharp gouged into her chest, a small metal claw tightening, followed by a terrible arcing pain from toe to crown, the world frying, filled with screams and smoke and pain, her own disembodied scream seeming to go on and on and on  and then nothing.

# CHAPTER FIFTEEN

Maria's eyes opened. Blurry, skipping like a run-out film reel, throbbing in time with her agitated heartbeat.

Richard stood over her, frowning. *Must be hallucinating . . . He's dead. Did they drug me?*

But his voice sounded harrowingly real. "You all right in there? Hope they didn't damage any circuits."

She felt hungover, the bodily trauma of a long night of drinking and smoking married with a deep, oppressive exhaustion. Speaking was like shards of glass being crunched beneath a boot into her brain tissue. "You're dead . . ."

The vision shook his head. "No, Maria. Not just

yet."

Her eyes peeled open wide. She tried to move her body but could not. She gazed down at her inert frame, willed herself to move, but could not. Her limbs felt stiff and paralysed, as if struck with rigor mortis. To her right sat Eva and Tāne. Tāne was mumbling unintelligibly, but Eva was still unconscious.

"Sorry about the tasers," Richard said. "A lot more powerful than the old sort. Extremely effective. The effect will wear off in a little while."

"Richard . . . What is this?" she mumbled.

"I'm sorry, Maria. It's just a precaution. I know you might be . . . confused. And angry."

"How—How are you still alive?"

Richard held up his arm and pointed to the underside of his forearm—the location of his subdermal implant. "I told you the automatic defences wouldn't target one of their own."

"But they did," Maria stammered. "Everybody around us died."

"*Everybody around us,* yes. You didn't, however. How do you think you survived?" The ghost of a smile traced his lips as he registered Maria's dawning horror. "I regret not being entirely forthcoming with you—I really didn't want all those people to die. And I'm sorry for not mentioning the lasers. But if I'd told you, nobody would have agreed to come, and I'd still be stuck in that rat's-nest you people call home."

"You . . . You killed them. Us. So many of us."

"Hey, I told you not to go charging in here," Richard said, frowning. "But you didn't listen, and more people got killed. That's on *you*."

"I don't understand," Maria said, her mind reeling, her confusion dwarfing her rage. "I felt you fall into the ocean, I thought you *died*—"

"It was a near thing, and a pretty mad gamble in hindsight," he admitted. "I knew the implant's signal would have registered with Central Control the moment we got within range that very first time—they knew I was alive." He smiled. "Then when I pinged with them the second time, during our invasion attempt, I figured they might glean what my return foreshadowed, my purpose. All risky bets and assumptions, but ultimately the gamble paid off. I had nothing left to lose, remember?

"After you were hit by the debris and knocked out—I presumed dead—I hid among the wreckage. After the retreat, once the dust settled, I swam into the quay and was met by allies who secretly brought me into the city and stashed me away. The Board knew nothing of my return."

"You—you told me all your supporters were executed, the leaders exiled."

Richard sighed. "A regrettable exaggeration. Many were executed and exiled, yes—but the Board knew too well the danger they courted, executing so many. There would be revolt—this time the whole city would be involved. So they stayed their hand. But it didn't stop the movement I started plotting away, their hate simmering.

"Fortunately for me, once I was back aboard and among my former collaborators, there were no power struggles; the temporary leadership abdicated without malice or bloodshed. I was back in my rightful place."

"Was this your plan all along?" Her rising anger took the edge from the stubborn pain in her head and body, almost soothing. "All those people, Richard . . . All those people, *my friends*, who trusted you and believed in you—"

"Again, regrettable," he replied earnestly. "But necessary for my vision."

"You piece of shit," Tāne slurred, stirring.

"I wasn't lying when I said I wanted to create a better world, a place of peace and security. You were right to hate the Board, Maria—that was our one unity of vision. The Board only cared about greed and profit, corrupting their new responsibility to the world—like Atlas, holding up the world and continued survival of humanity on his back—by the same business-as-usual bullshit. They *squandered* their opportunity to be leaders of men and abused their power."

"And I suppose you're a better fit?"

Richard smiled. "Don't misjudge me on account of the value I recognise in the Board's tactics. Our reasoning and moral bearing could not be more different. But it'd be foolish to disregard the compelling power of *fear*.

"I want peace and order, unity of purpose. That doesn't come from democracy, *people power*—it comes only when people are afraid. People don't really know what's good for them, individually speaking—and they certainly don't fathom the *common* good.

"The harsh and uncomfortable truth is, tyrannies are the most stable form of government, because people are too afraid to act or speak out. Life, survival, therefore, becomes a collective concern, rather than the individual concern of many: you obey and stay quiet because you endanger not only yourself, but your brothers and sisters; your family and comrades. Problematic trappings of individuality and self-interest become redundant, stripping them away even at the most primal level."

"I'm guessing that's why you teamed up with Guerrero and Fuckface over there, huh?" Tāne sneered, nodding his head towards Westfield, who stood against the far wall flanked by two East Prom soldiers, smiling.

Richard nodded. "I made a deal with Guerrero, of course. It was you who insisted how vital he was to our objective, and you were right—just not in the way you imagined. We shared the same vision for our communities."

"I bet," Tāne growled.

"Once I was aboard, I had word sent to Guerrero, who then sent additional support straight to the city—only this time, my allies in Central Security opened the gates and let them in."

"It was a slaughter," Maria guessed.

Richard sighed. "The military were firmly in the Board's pockets. We needed the additional forces to overwhelm them and oust the Board to consolidate our position. In exchange, I agreed to citizenship rights for all East Prom inhabitants, as well as a seat at the table for Guerrero."

Richard smiled at the surprised look on Maria and Tāne's faces. "I meant what I said, you know. I want peace and security—not just for Atlas-3, but the people struggling out in the Bay. I intend to extend the olive branch to your communities—Sunny Isle, Endurance Point, Kurunjang Port, the Marsh, and elsewhere. But boarding will be on the condition of total obedience, a commitment to the greater good—a preservation of order, at whatever cost." His smile broadened. "When bellies are growling, I hardly think they'll refuse."

"You sound like every story I ever heard about Tony," Maria said, her tone caustic. "You're perfect for each other."

Richard and Westfield exchanged a glance. "Actually, we've decided to cut Guerrero out of the equation."

Maria couldn't help but laugh. How had she misjudged Richard so badly? "What?"

"Guerrero only wants power for the sake of it. Power, in my eyes, is a necessary evil; a tool, for the betterment of mankind. I wield it grudgingly, but without scruple, to keep the people under my charge alive and safe. *Peace, no matter the cost.*"

"You're a fucking animal," Maria snarled.

Richard leaned down, his face inches away from hers. "All your talk of the greater good, and yet it was just for your own selfish interest. Vengeance is impotent without purpose, *real* purpose." He flashed an ugly smile. "It was never going to make your kids come back to life."

"Don't you *dare* mention my kids!"

"You blame me for all those lives lost, because I came up with the plan, but my vision, my purpose, was righteous—and I understood the sacrifices necessary to see it through. You, on the other hand, were happy to throw lives into the meat grinder just so you could exact the rage and vengeance you couldn't reconcile with your loss. All those deaths you blame on me, when you should be blaming yourself."

Maria spat in his face, her mouth twisted in rage.

"There's the Maria I know," Richard said smugly, wiping his face with his sleeve.

"So what now?" Tāne demanded.

"I'll have to execute you three, of course," Richard said. "Also a significant number of your entourage. It's not personal. But we must have a show of strength, to let citizens new and old know that disobedience, dissent and chaos won't be tolerated, if we are to have peace. The rest will be granted amnesty, so long as they accept our conditions. Once everything is secure here, we'll grant the same offer to your communities." His voice softened. "Don't worry, Maria, if they join me, they will be safe."

"You," Tāne said, looking first at Richard, then Westfield, "you're both a pair of dirty-ass snakes."

Suddenly, the glass-and-steel spire soaring above the Boardroom groaned. There was a massive, concussive rumble; the floor beneath them shook.

"What was that?" Westfield asked.

"It's just the storm," Richard replied, dismissive. "The city can handle it."

The city shook again, rocked to its foundations. This time, it was hard to ignore. That didn't sound like the storm—it sounded like an explosion.

Moments later, a loud siren began blaring across the city.

Richard unclipped a walkie-talkie on his belt and brought it to his mouth. "What's happening out there?"

"*Ships are approaching, sir! A whole fleet! They're attacking!*"

"Well, who the fuck are they?" Richard shouted back, glancing at Maria and Tāne suspiciously.

"*It's—it's East Prom, sir!*"

Richard's mouth fell open in horror. "What—"

"Looks like Tony might have suspected you were going to cut him out of the deal," Maria said, smiling.

"Or I've been double-crossed," Richard growled, reaching for his pistol.

Westfield's weapon was already out, levelled at Richard. The soldiers also had their weapons trained on him.

Richard chuckled, raising his hands. "I should have known. You ass-kissing little monkey."

"My loyalty to Mr Guerrero is unwavering. You underestimated and insulted his intelligence. You didn't think he *knew* you were going to try and screw him over?"

"I assumed he was too stupid to realise it had already happened."

"You assumed wrong. You're not fit to be leader. Atlas-3 is now under the stewardship of Antonio Guerrero." Westfield smiled unpleasantly. "Tell your people to surrender and power down the defences."

"No."

"No? Don't you realise that if you don't surrender, we will storm the city and kill every one of your people?"

"You'll be king of a city of ghosts," Richard replied, his eyes gleaming with mirth, "if you can get past the defences first."

While the others weren't looking, Maria flexed and unflexed her fingers. They moved rustily, like the legs of a dying spider, but they were moving, nonetheless. Feeling was returning to her body.

"Call your people," Westfield grated through clenched teeth, "and tell them to *shut—it—down*. Or we will sink this fucking place."

Richard's smile grew; he nodded towards the table. "The drawer. There's a remote. Turn the monitor on to channel five."

Westfield went to the desk. Finding the remote, he switched the TV above the boardroom desk on. He flicked through the channels, stopping at number five. A panorama of dark, churning seas, lit with bonfires, promptly snuffed out by seas splashing over decks, swallowing their crews, capsizing smoking derelicts. The smirking confidence evaporated from his face.

"You see, Westfield? You underestimated *me*. You are outmatched. The only reason any of you are standing here is because *I allowed it*. Such an idiotic crossing." Richard looked at Maria, shaking his head. "I knew it was you. I knew you wouldn't give up, and you didn't disappoint. Granted, your plan was smarter than trying to ride up to the gates a second time, fighting and dying, but you needn't have exhausted yourselves. I'd still have let you in. I *wanted* you to see what you'd helped create; the vision you had helped realise, even if not to its full and natural conclusion. You are scapegoats, after all—the final ingredient for securing my great peace."

He turned back to Westfield, his face bright with homicidal mischief. "All your men are going to die tonight, you treacherous piece of shit. And when the night is won, I will rain *hell* down on East Prom. I will cut Tony Guerrero's slimy head from his shoulders and make a ruin of his crappy empire."

Westfield fired. Richard dived to the boardroom floor as the bullet sailed into the wall, showering wooden splinters. Another gunshot—Westfield screamed, staggering and clutching his ankle. The two soldiers burst into action, one grabbing Westfield and pulling him back towards the door, the other rushing towards Richard's prostrate form.

Eva screamed, awake and alert, startled back to life by the gunshots.

Maria tipped her chair to the left, crashing into the path of the soldiers charging towards Richard. He fell against the wall with a surprised yelp. Tāne leapt to his feet, threw his chair aside and charged at Westfield and the other soldier, his movements like flowing water. His fist flew and connected with the soldier's jaw—then the man's submachine gun let out a muffled, buzzing volley.

Tāne staggered back, crimson flues in his back billowing red steam.

Maria grabbed the first soldier's gun and clubbed him on the brow, knocking him unconscious. She aimed the gun at the doorway, but Westfield and the other soldier had disappeared. A shining blood slick trailed in their wake.

"Tāne!" Maria and Eva rushed over to him. A great dark pool was forming beneath him.

Maria gingerly lifted his shirt, then covered her mouth. Tāne groaned, a long and bovine sound. It was bad, really bad—two through the stomach, two through his left kidney, one through his chest. An alarming pallor had already begun to take hold. A ghastly, shrill whistle emanated from the bullet-hole in his chest.

*He's going to die.*

Eva put both hands on Tāne's side, but he clenched, doubling over, roaring in agony. *"Don't,"* he gasped. "Let it be. It's over."

"No, you idiot," Maria said, tears spraying as she shook her head. "You have to live."

"Shut up, Maria," Tāne said, laughing weakly. "Stop being a dickhead. I'm done."

*"I can't lose you!* Not you!"

*"Stop Westfield."* He cupped Maria's face, smudging away a tear with his callused thumb, and smiled. "Save this place."

Then his hand slipped away and his eyes closed.

Maria buried her head in his bloodstained chest, her breathing heavy. Eva watched, her face hard but pale.

She laid a hand on Maria's shoulder.

"Maria," Richard's voice cut through the dismal silence. "I'm sorry about Tāne, he was a good man."

"You piece of shit," Maria laughed—a deranged, humourless sound. "Don't you dare say his name."

"You were going to kill him anyway," Eva snarled. "What do you care?"

"He would have made a good leader, if things had been different."

"He *was* a good leader," Maria snapped, full of hate. "You and Guerrero, however—two tyrants stabbing each other in the back, taking everybody else down with you. Real pieces of work, you are."

Richard held up his hands in surrender, laying his gun on the boardroom table. Maria rose to her feet, aiming the soldier's gun at his face.

"Eva, go down and find where they're keeping the others. We have to stop Westfield breaking into Central Security."

Eva nodded, snatching Richard's pistol from the table. "What about you?"

"Unfinished business." Maria's voice was heavy and cold.

Eva nodded, peered through the doorway, and disappeared. Maria and Richard stood alone in the boardroom.

"I will take this city back, you know," Richard said, as the room fell silent once more.

"No. You're done after this."

"The only way you'll stop me is by killing me," he said, smiling wickedly.

"I've killed men before."

"Not in cold blood. And not without recrimination. You're enslaved to your anger and hurt; worse, your guilt paralyses you. You're unwilling to do whatever's necessary to save your people, even if it means murder. You *can't*. Your conscience won't let you."

"I'm tempted."

"Well, go on, then. End it all now."

Maria flinched, realising how tightly her finger sat on the trigger—she hadn't even realised it had slidden down from the guard. Hate danced beneath her skin like a second skeleton, animating her limbs. Her finger tensed—but he was right, she couldn't do it.

She lowered the gun. "You're not worth the bullet. Nor the stain on my conscience."

The unconscious guard on the floor groaned, stirring. Maria's attention shifted for all of a split second, but that was all it took.

A moment later, a gunshot, spreading liquid fire

through her body.

Maria screamed, clutching her shoulder as she staggered, anger dissolving into shock and pain. A revolver—snatched from the small of his back, or from under the table—smoked in Richard's hand.

Her finger clamped around the trigger at last. The first burst went wide, screaming past him, blowing the glass out of the windows facing the atrium. The second volley found its mark, a zipper of red wounds like seeping eyes opening up from navel to throat. Richard pitched forward, gurgling.

She pushed herself upright, holding the table for balance. The slug ground on the bone, vexing the muscle around the shoulder blade. The smallest movements sparked intense bolts of pain. A little further to the right, it might have hit her spine and paralysed her. *Lucky*. The thought of being paralysed, having to listen to Richard goad and torment her anymore seemed worse than the paralysis itself.

The soldier was regaining consciousness. She took a step towards him and kicked him in the head, knocking him back out again. Then she went over to check on Richard.

He lay facing the ceiling, blood soaking into the blue carpet, his hair matted red against his scalp. His breaths were ebbing away; his eyes moved slowly in their sockets, gazing up her, pleading. His mouth opened and closed slowly like a suffocating goldfish, marooned out of its bowl.

She shook her head, pity overwhelming her. "You weren't worth the bullet. But you're also not worth saving."

She left him in his ill-gotten palace, bleeding all over the carpet for his few short moments of remaining life, alone.

# CHAPTER SIXTEEN

Outside in the corridors and atrium, the battle was raging fierce and bloody.

East Prom and Atlas-3 soldiers fired relentlessly at each other, almost indistinguishable—black uniforms firing on black. Bodies dropped here and there as the soldiers exchanged fire from behind retractable steel barricades in the floor. Explosions and powerful waves continued to rock the city from the outside.

Maria leapt down the stairs, grunting with pain, and ducked behind the statue of Atlas as a stray bullet ricocheted towards her. She ran down to the ground level and slid behind a barrier, right next to a trio of Atlas-3 soldiers. The closest one looked at her in surprise, then anger, turning his gun towards her.

"Wait! I'm not with East Prom!" she cried, raising her hands.

"No, you're just the ones that came with them!" His upper lip curled into a dog-like snarl. "Give me one good reason why I shouldn't kill you right now."

"*I'm not with them!* Please! Let me help you. We have to stop them!"

The soldier leaned over the edge of the barrier, let off a burst of shots, then ducked back down. "What the fuck do you think we're doing?"

"Richard is dead," she said.

"*What?*"

"Richard is dead. His tyranny is over."

The soldier blanched. "How the fuck does that help us, right now?"

"You don't need to fight for him anymore. You can fight with the people, your people, and us. We can stop East Prom together."

"Why the hell would we trust you?"

"What choice do you have? I don't trust you either, but I'm prepared to give it a try."

An explosion roared from one of the corridors, sending a wave of heat and screams into the atrium.

"Bloody maniacs!" the soldier roared in disbelief.

"How many people do you have left?"

The soldier cursed as a bullet whined past his head, as he peered over to take another shot. "Not enough. East Prom took us by surprise."

"Then let us help you. Let my people out. Call on the citizens to help defend their city."

Another explosion, this one closer, at the edge of the atrium. "*I can't!*"

"You can." She pointed to the name embroidered on his right breast, opposite the *A3* insignia: LT Dolasan. "Without a leader, in a crisis like this, you're probably the closest thing they have. You can turn the tide. Call it, or we all die."

A phalanx of East Prom soldiers advanced from the right corridor, their clear riot shields cracked from bullet impacts. They moved quickly, pausing and forming a kneeling shield wall at regular intervals as the Atlas-3 soldiers fired upon them, unwilling to surrender the atrium.

"*They're right on top of us,*" Maria cried. "End it, now!"

Dolasan ground his teeth, then snatched up his radio. "Control, this is Lieutenant Dolasan. Do you copy, over?"

*"Copy, Lieutenant, go ahead."*

"Requesting immediate release of mainland prisoners and issuing orders to *not* fire on them, repeat, *do not fire on mainland prisoners.* We require immediate assistance staving off East Prom forces, over."

*"Copy that, Captain. Request is denied. Prisoners are being detained on Governor Campbell's orders. Over."*

"Richard is dead, Control! I repeat, *Richard Campbell is dead.* East Prom is now our primary concern—we're losing men and we need help. I'm with their leader—What's your name?"

"Maria," she said.

"—Maria, who assures me they will cooperate. Requesting immediate release and re-arming of the mainland prisoners, with orders of non-engagement from Atlas-3 soldiers. Over!"

The radio was silent for a long time. Maria and Lieutenant Dolasan exchanged apprehensive looks, while bullets whined overhead and smacked into the barricade's plating. The gunfire was sounding closer than ever. Then: *"Wilco, Captain. Prisoner release is being supervised by Captain Ajani. Over."*

Dolasan exhaled with relief.

"More overhead!" someone yelled.

Maria peered around the barricade. East Prom

soldiers were sweeping along the mezzanine walkways, firing down into the barricades, pinning the Atlas-3 soldiers down.

"We can't hold them," Dolasan grated.

More East Prom soldiers entered from the left-hand corridor behind them. Maria's heart almost stopped. Now they were surrounded on all sides, and the enemy held the higher ground. Nowhere to run.

She glanced at Dolasan. The knowledge of defeat was written upon his face, long and heavy.

Gunfire broke out along the walkway above. East Prom soldiers screamed as unseen attackers fired into their ranks, mowing them down by the dozen. On the righthand side of the atrium, the East Prom soldiers fell, shouting in pain and alarm as they were flanked by Atlas-3 soldiers and men and women in wetsuits rushing up along the corridor.

Shocked by the sudden reversal, the East Prom soldiers facing Maria and Dolasan sneered and rose their guns to fire. At short range, there was no chance of escape.

A loud, collective roar swelled up from behind the soldiers—from the corridor, along the walkways, pealing out across the atrium and swallowing the city in defiant, chaotic noise. The soldiers turned to see a horde of well-dressed multitudes—men, mostly, but also a few women—armed with guns and makeshift melee weapons.

*The citizens of Atlas-3,* Maria realised in wonder. *They've rallied against them!*

The East Prom soldiers froze, their faces wrought with fear. The tide had turned, and disastrously fast.

They fired into the crowd as the human wave came rushing in, but Maria and Dolasan cut them down from behind before they could inflict too much damage.

The East Prom forces fell like dominoes all around the city. A short time later, the guns fell quiet, and silence fell once more over the halls of Atlas-3.

# EPILOGUE

"You didn't have to come, Maria."

Maria lowered her binoculars, flashing Eva a sour look. "I wanted to. I think Tony Guerrero needed the personal touch."

Eva nodded, then went back to staring down the long scope.

"Got him in sight yet?" Maria asked.

"If you keep pestering me, I'll miss it."

"Sorry." Maria resigned herself to the waiting game, staring interminably through the binoculars.

A flurry of movement on the southern side of the compound caught Maria's eye. "Down there!" she said, pointing. "South side, coming out the doors."

"I don't see him yet," Eva replied, a frown in her voice. "Just soldiers and—oh wait, there he is."

Eight soldiers in a rectangular formation around Guerrero, escorting him west.

"We've only got one shot at this, Eva. Make it count."

"They're moving too fast," Eva hissed. "That soldier on the right is blocking him."

"We can't lose him—"

"Shut up, Maria, I know!"

Eva took a long, deep breath. Her finger slid down, resting lightly on the trigger. She exhaled slowly, settling herself, adjusting her aim.

The bolt on the rifle snapped forward. The gunshot rang out across the escarpment, startling hidden flocks of birds into desperate flight.

Maria surveyed the ground. The soldiers were in disarray, shouting at one another, weapons drawn. The target at the centre lay on the ground, the top of his head sheered clean off.

Tony Guerrero was dead.

"Those birds will probably give us away," Eva said.

"Mm-hm. Time to boogie." Maria unclipped her

radio and pressed the talk button. "Lieutenant Dolasan, do you copy?"

"*Loud and clear, Maria. Over.*"

"Target is down, Lieutenant. You're clear to move in."

"*Copy that. We're converging on the docks now. Over.*"

"And Dolasan?"

"*Yes, Maria?*"

"Only kill the soldiers if you have to. We need to be better than them."

"*Roger that. Over.*"

\*\*\*

Dolasan escorted the East Prom refugees into the Atlas-3 atrium. Maria never got tired of the look of wonder and awe on the newcomers' faces as they entered the city's airlock. It brought a smile to her face to see their hope restored, drinking in the sights, the fact of things forgotten by years of hardship and hunger and oppression.

It would take most of their fleet and many round trips to get them all here, but the East Prom people would be a valuable addition to their ensemble. Many of the soldiers, too, had capitulated without contest, now that Guerrero, and Westfield, had been removed. Westfield had been found dead in an alleyway in Atlas-3's shopping precinct, his chest riddled with bullets. Without a head, the beast of East Prom flailed blindly. Their people were more than happy for a second chance, away from the memory of their hardship.

It would take the previous Atlas-3 citizens some time to acclimatise to mainland refugees. Even weeks since the first arrivals from Kurunjang and Endurance Point, some still turned their noses in the air, still baulked at the prospect of living side by side, as they once did before the Rise. Thankfully, after all the bloodshed and hostility, that was a minority—most people seemed content to put aside the past, grateful that their shared sacrifice had allowed them to go on breathing. Maria was optimistic things would only get better, even if the internal challenges morphed over time. She wasn't expecting an overnight miracle, nor for things to be smooth forever. She was under no illusions of the tensions of living in close quarters with others, learning to play nicely—but maybe this time, they'd do it better. Maybe a brave few had shown the rest how it could be done.

A funeral was held for the dead. Sunny Isle's new leader, Kaivao, a broad-bellied, heavily tattooed Tongan man and good friend of Tāne's, led a small coterie of men and women from the Isle to the city, dressed in black, wearing wreaths on their head. Visitors from all across the Bay and almost the entire city attended, watching from the spires and quays as the bodies were set out to sea. So many had given up their lives for the city that night: people, from the mainland and Atlas-3 alike, united in spilled blood—a covenant of their new friendship and unity.

Maria couldn't help wondering whether the prize was worth it.

She thought of Jeff, tearing up at the memory of shared blunts, his inept flirting; of Tāne's bear hugs and stupid lopsided smile.

Many called her a hero, but that wasn't true. She was simply the lesser evil with the nobler cause and had somehow won the day.

Even so, it was naïve to think people wouldn't find another reason to war again.

She thought of Abby, Deon and Luke. Would they be proud of what she had done, what it had cost?

Gosh, if they could only have seen this place.

But she couldn't live in the shadow of their memory, and her loss, anymore. The only way was forward. Atlas-3, and the new friendships surrounding her, had given and everybody else that chance to move on. To leave their ghosts behind.

Kaivao, Eva and Dolasan joined Maria up in the Boardroom after the funeral. She stared out the window, wrapped in a fetching black funeral gown, looking out over the sea.

"So you're the new boss now, huh?" Kaivao asked, rough-voiced and straight to the point.

Maria shook her head. "Only for the interim. I don't want it, anyway. Once all the refugees are aboard and things have settled down, we'll have nominations for a council and hold elections. We'll have a chancellor, but the position will always be accountable to the other members and to the city." She noticed Adnan's sour look and said, "It won't be like it was."

"All governments have said such things," he replied.

"It has to be different this time. *We* have to believe it'll be different this time, or else what was the point of it all? What is the point of going on?"

Adnan looked unconvinced; but he shrugged and nodded.

"We'll figure out the kinks, don't worry," Maria said, conciliatory.

"The word will have spread by now," Eva said

gravely. "The other lotus cities will know what's happened here and see you as a threat, a usurper. They're probably going to come after you. What will you do when they do?"

Maria gazed once more at the sea. The waves were calm now—the tides of war had subsided, and all was right with the world. Whether or not the peace would last . . . She hoped Eva was wrong. But if they did come . . .

Maria met her friend's eyes, her gaze cold and remote, then looked across the Strait, saying nothing.

# ABOUT THE AUTHOR

Marcus Turner is a speculative, horror, and dark fantasy author from Melbourne, Australia, where he lives with his wife Tita and his two children. He was first published in Deadset Press's *Beginnings* anthology with his story, "A Spark of Youth", in November 2018, and has since been featured in several other anthologies. He is a keen gamer, metalhead, avid reader of Batman and Judge Dredd comics, and is a little more obsessed with Cthulhu and all things Cthulhu Mythos than is probably healthy. Marcus cites Clive Barker, Stephen King, H.P. Lovecraft, Edgar Allen Poe, George R.R Martin and R. Scott Bakker as the major influences on his own writing. He is currently working on his first novel, entitled *Land of the Righteous*. You can connect with him via the following media:

Facebook: www.facebook.com/MarcusTurnerWriter/
Twitter: @FuryThePhoenix
Instagram: @marcusturnerauthor
Website: marcusturnerauthor.com

# ABOUT DEADSET PRESS

Deadset Press is the publishing imprint for Aussie
Speculative Fiction – a community aimed at supporting
Australian and Kiwi authors. You can learn more at:

www.aussiespeculativefiction.com

# ABOUT THE SERIES

*Drowned Earth is a series of eight standalone novellas, set in a shared world.*

### Prequel: Shards of Silver by Alanah Andrews
Debbie is on board a ship when an asteroid collides with Antarctica, causing a tsunami. And it's heading her way... (eBook Only: Free Download)

### The Rise by Sue-Ellen Pashley
The great Rise means that resources are scarce and not readily shared. But with her best friend's life at stake, along with some stranded refugees, Katie James knows she must prove there's more to being human than just existing. Even if that puts her on the same kill list.

### Fire Over Troubled Water by Nick Marone
Despite winds, torrential rains, storms, and bushfires, a fresh water merchant searches for his lost daughter among the autonomous island communities of flooded eastern New South Wales.

### Submerged City by Austin P. Sheehan
Melbourne is under martial law, overseen by general Messinger—an extremist who believes the flood is God's retribution against the left-wing agenda...

### Tides of War by Marcus Turner

After discovering a strange man in a row boat, Maria wages war on the lotus cities—clandestine floating communities off the coast of Victoria that are reserved for the wealthy.

### The Jindabyne Secret by Jo Hart

With nothing but a map and a rickety solar truck, Jax journeys to the top secret fresh water facility at Lake Jindabyne—one of the few fresh water lakes left in Australia. What he discovers there could be the key to saving his whole community, as long as the government doesn't kill him first.

### River of Diamonds by S. M. Isaac

Who would want to leave one of the last idyllic settlements since the Rise? Rosa has a map, a mercenary, and a hope to salvage a future for the world.

### Salvaged by C.A. Clark

Cassie lives in the safe haven of academics on the anchored city of new Melbourne. After a diving incident she is rescued by a territorial beach combing gang who trade goods washed up by the frequent storms. Cassie wishes she had never taken her home for granted.

### Emoto's Promise by Shel Calopa

Five hundred years after the flood, can Macie defeat the technology which has enslaved the last remaining humans in the walled city of Darwin?